John P Lockwood

Memorials of the Life of Peter Böhler

John P Lockwood

Memorials of the Life of Peter Böhler

ISBN/EAN: 9783337333287

Printed in Europe, USA, Canada, Australia, Japan

Cover: Foto ©Raphael Reischuk / pixelio.de

More available books at **www.hansebooks.com**

MEMORIALS OF THE LIFE

OF

PETER BÖHLER,

BISHOP OF THE CHURCH OF THE UNITED BRETHREN.

BY THE

REV. J. P. LOCKWOOD.

WITH AN INTRODUCTION

BY THE

REV. THOMAS JACKSON.

LONDON:

WESLEYAN CONFERENCE OFFICE,

2, CASTLE-ST., CITY-ROAD;

SOLD AT 66, PATERNOSTER-ROW.

1868.

LONDON:

PRINTED BY WILLIAM NICHOLS,

46, HOXTON SQUARE.

PREFACE.

THE following "Memorials" of one whose name is inseparably associated with the revival of spiritual religion in the early part of the eighteenth century are the result of careful and lengthened research. The outlines of them appeared several years ago, in a paper in the "Wesleyan-Methodist Magazine," at which time it was feared that no further authentic information respecting Peter Böhler could be procured. Having somewhat unexpectedly obtained access to the official archives of the Church at Herrnhut and Bethlehem, and other original authorities; and yielding to the wishes of friends whose judgment is entitled to respect; I have prepared a narrative which may not be wholly unacceptable to the religious public, and particularly to Wesleyan Methodists. I could easily have enlarged the volume from the store of unpublished materials in my possession; but, desirous to present a truthful and authentic record of such interesting events in a form conve-

A 2

nient and accessible to all, I have decided on confining the "Memorials" within their present limits.

My grateful acknowledgments are due, and are hereby presented, to several gentlemen who have favoured me with their welcome aid : especially to the Rev. Thomas Jackson, for his valuable "Introduction;" to the Revs. John Römer, and Edward von Schweinitz, the Archivarii at Herrnhut, and Bethlehem ; to the ecclesiastical and municipal authorities of several European cities for their courtesy and diligent researches ; to the Rev. Dr. Stevens, of New York, and the Rev. John Kirk, of Bristol, for important suggestions and other assistance; and to the Rev. A. C. Hasse, of London, and Mr. W. Tilburn, of Leeds, for their efficient services in translation and otherwise. Would that the volume, prepared amid engagements by no means light, had been more worthy of the memory of a servant of Christ so greatly to be revered ! It is now sent forth with the prayer that it may tend to promote the glory of our common Lord, and the spiritual interests of His Church.

SHIPLEY, NEAR LEEDS,
May 26th, 1868.

CONTENTS.

CHAPTER I.

CHAPTER II.

CHAPTER III.

CHAPTER IV.

CHAPTER V.

INTRODUCTION

IT has often pleased God to prepare by a course of severe discipline the men whom He has employed in eminent services, both in the world and the church; so that, in the midst of their elevation, they might remember their dependence upon Him, and ascribe the glory of their usefulness and exaltation to His unmerited goodness and sovereign will.

Before Joseph was endowed with the Spirit of prophecy, and was made a means of preserving the lives of thousands, and even ten thousands, of people, in a long time of famine, and thus obtained a popularity of which the world had scarcely seen an example, he was tried by exile, slavery, and imprisonment under a false accusation, and had a narrow escape from a violent and ignominious death.

Thus also Moses, before he was employed in leading the tribes of Israel out of Egypt, in performing a series of stupendous miracles, and in giving to God's chosen people their laws and ordinances, was

B

compelled to flee for his life ; and spent forty years
in a state of separation from his countrymen and
friends, and in the humble employment of a
shepherd.

Before David was raised to the throne of Israel,
and was employed in conducting a series of successful wars, as well as in making vast arrangements
for the public worship of Almighty God, he was
subjected to a long course of harassing persecution,
during which he was banished from the house of
God, and found it difficult to avoid a martyr's death.

Preparatory to his entrance upon his successful
career as the Apostle of the Gentiles, St. Paul was
deeply humbled by blindness, and by penitential
sorrow and terror, which, although they were not of
any long continuance, left an impression of which
he could never divest himself during the subsequent
years of his eventful life. Never did he forget what
he passed through in the three days and nights
which he spent at Damascus, when " he did neither
eat nor drink," was deprived of sight, and was
uncertain whether his final doom would be forgiveness or condemnation, heaven or hell.

The case of Luther was somewhat similar. As a
preparation for his entrance upon the great work of
Reformation, he had most distressing and even
agonizing views of the natural sinfulness of his
heart, of his guilt in the sight of God, and of his
consequent liability to suffer the vengeance of eternal fire. His paroxysms of grief and alarm were at

times so deep and overwhelming, and his strength
was so exhausted by fasting, abstinence, and prayer,
that speedy death appeared to be inevitable.
It was the relief which he obtained by faith in the
blood of the Cross, that corrected the theological
errors of his education, and nerved him for the
difficult and perilous work of assailing the enormous
errors and abuses of the Papacy. But for his religious experience, there is no reason to believe that
he would ever have assumed the character of a
Reformer. He felt that Popery interferes with the
salvation of the souls of men ; and hence his heroic
and untiring efforts to overthrow its leading tenets.

The case of the Rev. John Wesley bears a
strong resemblance to the cases now mentioned.
Few men since the apostolic times have been more
successful than he in promoting true spiritual religion in the world ; and, to qualify him for the course
of labour to which he was providentially called, he
passed through a long preparatory training of a
painful and humiliating kind, which left upon his
character an indelible impress. His early education
devolved mostly upon his gifted mother ; who taught
him, in connexion with the elements of literature, to
say his prayers at certain specified times ; to believe
all the articles of the Christian faith, as they are
embodied in the three Creeds ; to keep the command-
ments ; to fear God ; and to observe all the rules of
morality, and of a strict decorum. These lessons
were not lost upon him, but were exemplified in his

general deportment; so that he was a diligent student and an obedient son; and when he had passed through his academical course, he was an accomplished scholar, a man of correct morals, and an agreeable companion. He was an acute logician, well read in philosophy, familiar with the Greek and Latin languages; and he possessed also a knowledge of Hebrew, Arabic, and French. With these accomplishments he afterwards combined an acquaintance with the German, Italian, and Spanish.

At the age of twenty-two he was ordained deacon; and then, under the direction of his father, entered upon the study of divinity, with a reference both to his pulpit labours, and the regulation of his personal conduct. But, unhappily for him, instead of studying the Bible, in connexion with the writings of the master spirits of Protestant Christendom, he was led into a course of reading which, in his then state of mind, served only to perplex and confound him, and that through a series of anxious years. Four volumes occupied his special attention: Kempis's "Christian's Pattern," Bishop Taylor's "Rules and Exercises of Holy Living and Dying," and William Law's treatise on "Christian Perfection," and his "Serious Call to a Devout and Holy Life." To most of these works he took exceptions in the first instance, and carried on a correspondence respecting them with his father and mother, thinking them too strict in their requirements. But as he persevered in the study of them, he assented to their teaching, and in the name of God resolved to exemplify their principles in his own daily practice.

From Kempis he learned that true religion consists especially in a right state of the heart, being an exact conformity in spirit and in action to the example of the Lord Jesus Christ, maintained by habitual intercourse with Him. Kempis was a monk, separated from the cares of active and public life; and his volume bears indubitable marks of an ascetic character.

From Bishop Taylor Mr. Wesley learned especially that it is the duty of Christians to serve God with constant simplicity of purpose; so that whether they eat or drink, converse, engage in the ordinary duties of life, are employed in acts of devotion, or whatever they do, they ought to set the Lord before them, and aim simply to glorify Him by an entire compliance with His will. " In every action," says his Lordship, " reflect upon the end ; and in your undertaking it consider why you do it, and what you propound to yourself for a reward. Begin every action in the name of the Father, of the Son, and of the Holy Ghost."

William Law was a clergyman of the Church of England; and as he was then living, Mr. Wesley formed a personal acquaintance with him, and received his instructions with profound deference ; for Law was a man of great gravity, of unquestionable

scholarship and genius, and affected to speak on
religious subjects in a tone of even oracular authority. Being attached to the Stuart dynasty, and
unwilling to take the oath of allegiance to the
reigning monarch, he was incapable of holding any
living in the Established Church, and was known
rather as an author than a preacher. He was a somewhat voluminous writer, and in the latter years of
his life advocated the mysterious dogmas of Jacob
Behmen. But his two volumes just mentioned
may be justly ranked among the most powerful and
impressive works of the kind that ever appeared in
the English language; and they were extensively
read at the time of their publication. They expose,
with unsparing severity, the ungodliness of the age.
They show that Christianity admits of no com-
promise with worldliness and sin. The author
insists upon the absolute necessity of entire devoted-
ness to God from the beginning of life to the end;
inasmuch as this is the great purpose of human
existence, as well as of the manifestation of the Son
of God in the flesh, and especially of His death upon
the cross, and is the appointed way to happiness in
a future state. Considering the shortness and un-
certainty of life, and the momentous consequences
which depend upon the manner in which it is spent,
he shows that nothing can surpass the folly of those
ladies who employ their time in dress and in
fashionable amusements, to the neglect of personal
godliness, offering to the Lord their Maker nothing

more than an occasional and formal worship; and
that the men who spend their days in the mere
accumulation of wealth, or in such studies as
neither tend to the glory of God, nor the benefit of
mankind, but only the gratification of a vain
curiosity,—never aiming at a resemblance to their
Saviour, nor at any kind of worship but that which
is merely external,—act a part which is equally vain
and sinful. He asks what difference it can make to
the immortal spirit of a dying man whether he has
accumulated, and is prepared to leave to his heir,
a hundred thousand pounds, or a hundred thousand
pairs of boots and spurs. Law is a fine writer, in
respect both of sentiment and style. His diction is
thoroughly English; and the numerous characters
which he has sketched, in illustration of the different subjects he has introduced, are delineated in a
manner consummately beautiful, showing in every
touch the hand of a master. "When at Oxford,"
says Dr. Johnson, "I took up Law's 'Serious Call
to a Devout and Holy Life,' expecting to find it a dull
book, (as such books generally are,) and perhaps to
laugh at it. But I found Law quite an overmatch for
me: and this was the first occasion of my thinking in
earnest of religion after I became capable of rational
inquiry." Law lived some time at Putney, in the
neighbourhood of London, where he was visited by
the Wesleys, when prosecuting their religious
inquiries. The latter years of his life were spent at
Thrapston, in Northamptonshire. A short biography

of him by Mr. Richard Tighe was published in the year 1813.

All the works just mentioned Mr. Wesley not only read, but carefully studied, as his correspondence with his parents clearly shows. But Law was evidently his favourite author. He laboured with ceaseless assiduity to exemplify Law's doctrine in every part of his own conduct; and Law's views of religion formed the staple of his public ministrations. It may indeed be questioned, whether the writer of the " Serious Call " had in the entire kingdom another disciple who was equally docile and zealous.

Every morning he rose at the early hour of four o'clock, and so apportioned his time to his engagements, that scarcely a moment was without its appropriate occupation. He reduced his personal expenditure to the smallest possible amount, and applied the remainder of his money to objects of religion and charity, regarding himself simply in the light of a steward. Remembering that for every idle word that men utter they must give an account in the day of judgment, he resolved to confine his conversation to sacred subjects, and to matters of real utility. He sought for religious companions, and made arrangements with them for regular meetings in order to their mutual improvement, especially in personal godliness. He adopted the fasts of the early Church, abstaining from all food every Wednesday and Friday, till three o'clock in the .

afternoon. He spent much time in secret devotion, attended all the ordinances of public worship, and received the Lord's Supper every week. At the same time, he visited the prisoners in the jail, for the purpose of religious instruction and prayer; and, with the aid of his friends, he supported a school for the education of poor and neglected children; seeking also to promote the spiritual and moral benefit of all the persons with whom he was brought into intercourse, by calling their attention to a future state of retribution, and the importance of a due preparation for it. Being regularly employed as a college tutor, he was especially careful to imbue his pupils with the true fear of God, and a love of His holy Name.

While his outward conduct was thus regulated by the strictest rules of morality and religion, he was equally attentive to all the movements of the inner man ; subjecting himself, at stated times, to a severe scrutiny as to his thoughts, desires, emotions, and intentions, in every employment, whether religious or secular, and in all the circumstances through which he passed.* His habitual prayer seemed to be, " What I know not, teach Thou me ; " and, " Search me, O God, and know my heart : try me, and know my thoughts : and see if there be any wicked way in me, and lead me in the way everlasting."

A fact which he has related relative to the expenditure of his money will show his conscientious-

* Works, vol. xi., pp. 514–516, edit. 1830.

ness in this respect. "Many years ago," says he, "when I was at Oxford, in a cold winter's day, a young maid (one of those we kept at school) called upon me. I said, 'You seem half-starved. Have you nothing to cover you but that thin linen gown?' She said, 'Sir, this is all I have.' I put my hand in my pocket; but I found I had scarce any money left, having just paid away what I had. It immediately struck me, 'Will thy Master say, Well done, good and faithful steward?—Thou hast adorned thy walls with the money which might have screened this poor creature from the cold! O justice! O mercy! Are not these pictures the blood of this poor maid?' —See thy expensive apparel in the same light; thy gown, hat, head-dress! Every thing about thee which cost more than Christian duty required thee to lay out is the blood of the poor! O, be wise for the time to come! Be more merciful, more faithful to God and man, more abundantly adorned (like men and women professing godliness) with good works!" *

So intent was he, at this period of his life, upon attaining to the highest degrees of personal godliness, that he withstood the importunity of his friends, who urged him to apply for the rectory of Epworth, which was likely soon to become vacant, his father being aged, and in a declining state of health; alleging that he had greater facilities for the cultiva-

* Sermons, vol. iii., p. 23, edit. 1805.

tion of religious habits as a resident Fellow of a college, than he should have in a country parish; and that the more holy he was in himself, the greater would be his usefulness in his peculiar calling. There is an indication of great sincerity in his reasonings on this subject; but neither he nor his friends saw the ultimate bearing of his present resolution. He was destined to spend the better part of his life neither in the cloisters of Oxford, nor within the limits of a parochial charge, but as an evangelist of the United Kingdom. As to his conduct in the meanwhile, he made the following appeal from the pulpit of the University, after he had ceased to reside in one of its colleges. Having described the character of the man who is almost, but not altogether, a Christian, he says: " I did go thus far for many years, as many of this place can testify; using diligence to eschew all evil, and to have a conscience void of offence; redeeming the time; buying up every opportunity of doing all good to all men; constantly and carefully using all the public and all the private means of grace; endeavouring after a steady seriousness of behaviour, at all times and in all places: and, God is my record, before whom I stand, doing all this in sincerity; having a real design to serve God; a hearty desire to do His will in all things; to please Him who had called me to ' fight the good fight,' and to ' lay hold of eternal life.' " *

* Sermons, vol. i., p. 22, edit. 1865.

While he was thus exerting himself to exemplify the " rules and exercises of holy living " supplied by Bishop Taylor, and cultivating the ascetic piety recommended by William Law, he was requested to go abroad as a missionary to the American Indians bordering upon the colony of Georgia, then recently formed. With this application he complied, believing the call to be providential, and thinking that in the new mode of life upon which it was proposed that he should enter, he would not only serve the cause of Christ among the heathen, but also escape from the temptations by which he was beset in polished society, gratify the yearning that he felt after pious solitude, and minister to an unsophisticated people, who would receive the Gospel as little children.

In these hopes he was disappointed ; for, on his arrival in the colony, the clergyman in charge of the settlers resigned his office, and Mr. Wesley was requested to supply his place till another appointment should be made. During his stay in Georgia he repeatedly applied to be released from the office which he sustained among the English, that he might enter upon his mission, but was as often denied by the Governor, who pleaded the claims of the settlement, which in the event of his departure would be left without the ordinances of religion. He therefore remained in the colony, where he was ill-requited for his services in behalf of those whose benefit it was his earnest desire to promote.

When he went to Georgia he was accompanied by

his brother Charles, who had long entertained the same views of religion, and with whom he was one in mind and heart. Charles lived at Frederica, with Oglethorpe, the Governor, to whom he sustained the relation of secretary, officiating, at the same time, as a clergyman among the people who were resident there. John lived at Savannah, where the emigrants mostly resided. Oglethorpe was generous and enterprising. It was by his means especially that the imprisoned debtors of London were liberated, and the colony formed for their accommodation. He highly appreciated the character of the Wesleys, and upon the whole treated them with becoming respect; but in a few instances he listened to sinister whisperings to their disadvantage, and withdrew from them a confidence to which they were justly entitled. Of these occasional fits of ill-humour he appears to have been afterwards heartily ashamed, and made honourable amends by treating the two brothers to the end of his protracted life with the utmost deference, as men of intelligence, and of unquestionable integrity.

Mr. Wesley remained upwards of two years in Georgia; and, during the whole of this time, he laboured with undiminished assiduity to attain to a right state of heart, and to fulfil the obligations under which he lay both to God and man. As a clergyman, he acted in strict accordance with the rubric contained in the Book of Common Prayer; baptizing children by immersion, unless their parents declared them to be in delicate health; and refusing the Lord's Supper to all persons, whether rich or poor, men or women, whose conduct was matter of public offence, who had given no signs of repentance, and who neglected to give notice beforehand of their intention to appear at the Lord's table. At the same time, his sermons were characterized by a stern morality, and the enforcement of a rigid self-denial, such as Kempis and William Law regarded as essential to Christianity.

These things, it is easy to imagine, were very distasteful to the people, among whom were Dissenters, who liked neither the Prayer-Book nor its rubrics. Many others had just escaped from the London prisons, having little or no sense of religion, and whose spirits were chafed by the hard labour to which they were compelled to submit, in a climate much warmer than that of England. The mystical philosophy of Law which they heard from the pulpit they did not understand; and the earnest enforcement of moral duties they felt to be a censure upon their vices. Hardly any one of them formed a right estimate of the man who thus laboured among them. They had no just apprehension of his sincerity, and of his intense desire to promote their best interests. He was upright and single-minded, but mistaken, and " working in chains," which he knew not how to break: yet who can forbear to admire the honesty of the man who, from conscientious motives, had resigned the pleasures of polite society, and the learned leisure of a college, to live in a wilderness, in the midst of spies, friendless, except when he had a casual interview with his brother, or visited the godly Moravians in the neighbourhood ; being sometimes for months together without a shilling in his pocket, wasting his strength among a thankless and gainsaying people ?

In the midst of these grave discouragements he steadily persevered in the fulfilment of his clerical duties ; the onerous nature of which may be judged of from the bare mention of his Sabbath services, of which he gives the following record in his Journal, under the date of October 30th, 1737 :— " The first English prayers lasted from five till half-an-hour past six. The Italian (which I read to a few Vaudois) began at nine. The second service for the English (including the sermon and the Holy Communion) continued from half-an-hour past ten, till about half-an-hour past twelve. The French service began at one. At two I catechized the children. About three began the English service. After this was ended, I had the happiness of joining with as many as my largest room would hold, in reading, prayer, and singing praise. And about six the service of the Moravians, so called, began ; at which I was glad to be present, not as a teacher, but a learner."

On the week-days he read prayers and expounded the second lesson every morning at five o'clock, dismissing the people to their work before six.

Every evening he had a similar service at seven o'clock, when the worldly labours of the day were ended.

Among his adversaries at Savannah two men were specially distinguished,—Mr. Causton, the storekeeper, and Mr. Williamson, who had married Causton's niece. They commenced a suit against him in the civil court; but, when he attended to meet the charges and to defend himself, the matter was deferred. Seeing that their object was annoyance, and not the redress of any real grievance, he gave public notice that he should return to England, no one offering any opposition, except by words. The real character of the men who had begun this suit soon after appeared. Causton was prosecuted for an embezzlement of public money; and Williamson fled clandestinely from the colony, to avoid the consequences of more grave offences. Men of their character, it will be at once perceived, had sufficient reasons for wishing to get rid of such a man as Mr. Wesley, whose preaching and example were a perpetual reproof to all workers of iniquity. With such men complaints against him on account of his high and intolerant Churchmanship were a mere pretence.

The state of mind most of all to be dreaded by a professed Christian is that of assuming that he is "rich and increased" in spiritual and moral "goods," so that he has "need of nothing;" when the truth is, that he is "wretched, and miserable,

and poor, and blind, and naked." Happily for Mr.
Wesley, he was preserved from this dangerous delu-
sion. During his voyage home he instituted a strict
inquiry into his state in respect of religion, and
came to the conclusion that his heart was not right
in the sight of God. However blameless his conduct
might appear in the sight of men, and whatever
might be his zeal and activity in the service of God, he
had neither the happiness nor the inward purity of
a true believer in Christ. His mind was restless
and uneasy; he was afraid to die; and he was
under the dominion of inward sin, especially the sin
of unbelief, of pride, of irrecollection, and of levity.
His mind wandered from God; "vain thoughts
lodged within" him; he was led into airy and
useless speculations; and, sometimes, he not only
doubted whether there is a future state, and whether
the Bible is true, but whether there really is a God, or
not. Referring to his state at this period of his
life, he says, in one of his sermons, "After heaping
up the strongest arguments which I could find,
either in ancient or modern authors, for the very
being of a God, and (which is nearly connected
with it) the existence of an invisible world, I have
wandered up and down, musing with myself: 'What,
if all these things which I see around me, this earth
and heaven, this universal frame, have existed from
eternity? What, if the generation of men be
exactly parallel with the generation of leaves?—if
the earth drops its successive inhabitants, just as

the tree drops its leaves ?   What, if that saying of a
great man be really true,—

> Death is nothing, and nothing is after death?

How am I sure that this is not the case; that I have
not followed cunningly-devised fables ?'   And I have
pursued the thought, till there was no spirit in me,
and I was ready to choose strangling rather than
life." *

He was equally unsuccessful in his attempts to
obtain the lively and joyous hope of a blessed im-
mortality, to which believers in Christ are "begotten
again."   "How often have I laboured," says he,
"and that with my might, to beget this hope in
myself!   But it was lost labour: I could no more
acquire this hope of heaven, than I could touch
heaven with my hand.   And whoever makes the
same attempt, will find it attended with the same
success.   I do not deny, that a self-deceiving enthu-
siast may work in himself a kind of hope; he may
work himself up into a lively imagination, into a
sort of pleasing dream; he may 'compass himself
about,' as the prophet speaks, 'with sparks of his
own kindling:' but this cannot be of long continuance; in a little while the bubble will surely break.
And what will follow?   'This shall ye have at My
hand, saith the Lord, ye shall lie down in sorrow.'" †

He was no less disappointed in his efforts to
produce in himself that love to God and man, which

---

* Sermons, vol. ii., pp. 405, 406, edition of 1865.

† *Ibid.*, p. 407.

is the end of the commandment, and therefore the principle of all holiness. " But what," says he, " can cold reason do in this matter ? It may present us with fair ideas ; it can draw a fine picture of love : but this is only a painted fire. And farther than this reason cannot go. I made the trial for many years. I collected the finest hymns, prayers, and meditations which I could find in any language ; and I said, sung, or read them over and over, with all possible seriousness and attention. But still I was like the bones in Ezekiel's vision : ' the skin covered them above ; but there was no breath in them.' " *

When returning to England, upon the bosom of the great deep, his " mind was full of thought," and, in the fulness of his heart, he made the following entry in his private journal :—" I went to America to convert the Indians ; but O ! who shall convert me ? who, what is he that will deliver me from this evil heart of unbelief ? I have a fair summer religion. I can talk well ; nay, and believe myself, while no danger is near : but let death look me in the face, and my spirit is troubled. Nor can I say, ' To die is gain.'

> ' I have a sin of fear, that when I've spun
> My last thread, I shall perish on the shore.'

" I think, verily, if the Gospel be true, I am safe : for I not only have given, and do give, all my goods to feed the poor ; I not only give my body to be burned, drowned, or whatever God shall appoint for

* Sermons, vol. ii., p. 409.

c 2

me; but I follow after charity, (though not as I ought, yet as I can,) if haply I may attain it. I *now* believe the Gospel is true. I show my faith by my works, by staking my all upon it. I would do so again and again a thousand times, if the choice were still to make. Whoever sees me, sees I would be a Christian. Therefore are my ways not like other men's ways. Therefore I have been, I am, I am content to be, 'a by-word, a proverb of reproach.' But in a storm I think, 'What, if the Gospel be not true? Then thou art of all men most foolish. For what hast thou given thy goods, thy ease, thy friends, thy reputation, thy country, thy life? For what art thou wandering over the face of the earth? —A dream, a cunningly-devised fable!' O! who will deliver me from this fear of death? What shall I do? Where shall I fly from it!"

A few days after making this record, he landed in England, and said, "It is now two years and almost four months since I left my native country, in order to teach the Georgian Indians the nature of Christianity: but what have I learned myself in the mean time? Why, (what I least of all suspected,) that I, who went to America to convert others, was never myself converted to God. 'I am not mad,' though I thus speak; but 'I speak the words of truth and soberness;' if haply some of those who still dream may awake, and see, that as I am, so are they.

"Are they read in philosophy? So was I. In

ancient or in modern tongues? So was I also. Are they versed in the science of divinity? I too have studied it many years. Can they talk fluently upon spiritual things? The very same could I do. Are they plenteous in alms? Behold, I gave all my goods to feed the poor. Do they give of their labour, as well as of their substance? I have laboured more abundantly than they all. Are they willing to suffer for their brethren? I have thrown up my friends, reputation, ease, country; I have put my life in my hand, wandering into strange lands; I have given my body to be devoured by the deep, parched up with heat, consumed by toil and weariness, or whatsoever God should please to bring upon me. But does all this (be it more or less, it matters not) make me acceptable to God? Does all I ever did or can know, say, give, do, or suffer, justify me in His sight? Yea, or the constant use of all the means of grace? (Which, nevertheless, is meet, right, and our bounden duty.) Or that I know nothing of myself; that I am as touching outward moral righteousness blameless? Or (to come closer yet) the having a rational conviction of all the truths of Christianity? Does all this give me a claim to the holy, heavenly, divine character of a Christian? By no means. If the oracles of God are true, if we are still to abide by 'the law and the testimony;' all these things, though, when ennobled by faith in Christ, they are holy and just and good, yet, without it, are as 'dung and dross,' meet only to be purged away by 'the fire that never shall be quenched.'

"This, then, I have learned in the ends of the earth, That I am fallen short of the glory of God; that my whole heart is altogether corrupt and abominable; and consequently my whole life; (seeing it cannot be, that an evil tree should bring forth good fruit;) that, alienated as I am from the life of God, I am a child of wrath, an heir of hell; that my own works, my own sufferings, my own righteousness, are so far from reconciling me to an offended God, so far from making any atonement for the least of those sins, which are more in number than the hairs of my head, that the most specious of them need an atonement themselves, or they cannot abide His righteous judgment; that, having the sentence of death in my heart, and having nothing in or of myself to plead, I have no hope but that of being justified freely 'through the redemption that is in Jesus.' I have no hope, but that if I seek I shall find Christ, and 'be found in Him, not having my own righteousness, but that which is through the faith of Christ; the righteousness which is of God by faith.' " *

When Mr. Wesley returned from America, in the year 1738, he had been in the Christian ministry some twelve or thirteen years; and during the whole of this time he was an example of diligence in the

Journal.

discharge of his clerical duties, and used every means that he could devise to attain to a state of sincere and confirmed piety. He fasted, he prayed in secret, he attended all the public means of grace, and endeavoured to promote the spiritual benefit of all who were brought within the range of his influence. It is therefore natural to inquire why it is that, after all he had done and suffered, he should so far fall short of the Christian character, as we find it described in the New Testament. According to the apostolical Epistles, believers in Christ are a happy people; they exhibit in their daily walk "the fruit of the Spirit;" they are free from the dominion of sin; they are delivered from the fear of death, and they rejoice in hope of the glory of God. How is it then that Mr. Wesley, after the incessant labour of more than twelve years, should be in the lamentable state he has described in terms of such deep pathos? We believe the true reason is to be found in the words of the apostle: "Israel, which followed after the law of righteousness, hath not attained to the law of righteousness. Wherefore? Because they sought it not by faith, but as it were by the works of the law." (Rom. ix. 31, 32.)

According to the teaching of Holy Scripture, the state of all mankind, both by nature and practice, is a state of *guilt* and *depravity;* of *condemnation* and of *utter sinfulness.* Their sinfulness renders them unfit for heaven, and their guilt exposes them to the endless miseries of hell. Every man, therefore,

stands in absolute need of the double blessing of
justification and sanctification; understanding by
these terms the full and free forgiveness of all past
sin, and the renewal of the heart in righteousness
and true holiness. These blessings constitute the
"great salvation" provided for mankind by the
mediation of Christ, revealed in the Gospel, and
offered to men in the present world. These most
gracious gifts of God are distinct in their nature, but
inseparably connected; so that every justified man is
in part sanctified, and every sanctified man is justified. Yet, in the order of nature and of thought,
justification precedes sanctification: for until a man
is justified, he is under the sentence of death; he is
"condemned already," and "the wrath of God
abideth on him." (John iii. 18, 36.) While he
remains in this state, we cannot conceive of the
Holy Spirit as sanctifying him, so as to make him a
partaker of the Divine nature. But when the act
of justification takes place, so that the man is
no longer under condemnation, there is no legal bar
in the way of the Holy Spirit's operation; and
hence the new creation immediately follows, and the
man in a two-fold sense "passes from death unto life."
Personal justification, therefore, lies at the foundation of all sound Christian experience; it is the
basis and commencement of the Christian life. It
formed one of the principal subjects of the apostolic
ministry, and was realized in every Christian convert, both Jew and Greek.

Our blessed Saviour taught the doctrine of present justification by faith in the course of His personal ministry. The publican whom He describes as going in a state of conscious guilt to the temple, and there smiting upon his breast, in an agony of penitential grief, and praying, " God be merciful to me a sinner," " *went down to his house justified,*" having actually obtained the blessing of pardoning mercy upon which his heart was set. (Luke xviii. 13, 14.) To the woman that was a sinner, who washed His feet with her tears, and wiped them with the hairs of her head, He said, " *Thy sins are forgiven. Thy faith hath saved thee :* go in peace." (Luke vii. 48, 50.)

After His resurrection our Lord directed His apostles to preach " repentance and *remission of sins* in His name among all nations, beginning at Jerusalem." (Luke xxiv. 47.) Accordingly, St. Peter, in opening his commission on the day of Pentecost, cried to the assembled multitudes, " Repent, and be baptized every one of you in the name of Jesus Christ *for the remission of sins,* and ye shall receive the gift of the Holy Ghost." (Acts ii. 38.) Aware of the importance of this doctrine, he added, a few days afterwards, " Repent ye therefore, and be converted, *that your sins may be blotted out.*" (Acts iii. 19.) Still true to his calling, the same apostle, addressing Cornelius and his friends, said in reference to Christ, " To Him give all the prophets witness, that through His Name *whosoever believeth*

in Him shall receive remission of sins." (Acts x. 43.)
To the Jews at Antioch, in Pisidia, St. Paul said,
" Be it known unto you,...that through this Man is
preached unto you *the forgiveness of sins:* and by Him
all that believe are justified from all things, from
which ye could not be justified by the law of Moses."
(Acts xiii. 38, 39.) St. Paul also states that the
purpose of his mission to the Gentiles was, that he
might "turn them from darkness to light,...that
they might *receive the forgiveness of sins."* (Acts
xxvi. 18.)

The converted people who formed the various
churches to whom the apostles addressed their
Epistles are all spoken of as having received this
great blessing at the hands of God, and as living in
the enjoyment of it, unless they had drawn back
from their allegiance to Christ, and their faith in
Him. To the Romans St. Paul said, " *Being justified by faith,* we have peace with God through our
Lord Jesus Christ." (Rom. v. 1.) To the Corinthi-
ans: " *Ye are justified* in the name of the Lord
Jesus." (1 Cor. vi. 11.) To the Galatians: "We
have believed in Jesus Christ, that we might be
justified by the faith of Christ." (Gal. ii. 16.) To the
Ephesians: " *We have redemption through His blood,
the forgiveness of sins."* (Eph. i. 7.) The Philip-
pians he assumes to be living in a state of conscious
reconciliation with God through the mediation of
Christ; and therefore says to them, " *Rejoice in the
Lord* alway: and again I say, *Rejoice."* (Phil. iv. 4.)

To the Colossians he writes, "*We have redemption through His blood, even the forgiveness of sins.*" (Col. i. 14.) The Thessalonians he exhorts to "*rejoice evermore;*" (1 Thess. v. 16;) which it was impossible for them to do, unless they had an assurance of their acceptance with God through the atonement of His Son. The Hebrews he addresses as "partakers of the heavenly calling;" and declares that God, in accordance with the provisions of the Christian covenant, has said, "I will be merciful to their unrighteousness, *and their sins and their iniquities will I remember no more.*" (Heb. viii. 12.) St. Peter addresses the Christians of his day, who were widely dispersed through different countries, as a people who had "*obtained mercy,*" and who, believing in Christ, rejoiced in Him "*with joy unspeakable and full of glory.*" (1 Peter i. 8; ii. 10.) St. John divides the Christians whom he addresses into three classes: "little children," "young men," and "fathers;" and to the lowest of these divisions he says, "I write unto you, little children, *because your sins are forgiven you* for His name's sake." (1 John ii. 12.)

The great doctrine of present justification, through faith in the blood of Christ, which is thus prominent in the Christian Scriptures, was one of the leading doctrines of the Protestant Reformers, and is explicitly asserted in the formularies of the Church of England; which declares in her eleventh Article, "We are accounted righteous before God, only for the merit of our Lord and Saviour Jesus Christ by faith, and not for our own works or deservings : Wherefore, that *we are justified by faith only* is a most wholesome doctrine, and very full of comfort, as more largely is expressed in the Homily on Justification." Yet it has too often happened that doctrines which are prominent in Creeds and Confessions of Faith are seldom or never heard from the pulpit. So it has been in the Church of England with respect to the vital doctrine of justification by faith. It was so modified, and explained away, by such writers as Dr. Hammond, Bishop Taylor, Bishop Bull, and Dr. Waterland, that scarcely any trace of it was to be found in the popular teaching of the English clergy at the time of Mr. Wesley's ordination. It may be fairly doubted, whether in any parish-church in England, at that time, this doctrine was statedly, and of set purpose, expounded and enforced. The attention of the writer of these remarks has long been directed to this subject ; and he confesses his inability to specify a single example of the kind. It is not, therefore, surprising that this momentous truth escaped Mr. Wesley's attention when he entered upon his ministry. He might, however, have found it both in the Prayer-Book and the New Testament, had he been duly attentive to the subject. The doctrine might also have been found in volumes published by Nonconformist ministers ; but these the prejudices of his education would not allow him to read ; and, had he read them, he would have been justly offended to find the doctrine in question placed in direct connexion with the theory of partial redemption, and of absolute election and reprobation.

Mr. Wesley, as we have already observed, studied theology with a reference not merely to his public ministry, but to the regulation of his personal conduct ; and it was his misfortune that his attention was specially directed to Kempis, Taylor, and Law : men whose works maybe read with great advantage by spiritually-minded persons of evangelical views ; but are most misleading to those who know not the way of life, and are prosecuting the inquiry, " What must I do to be saved?" All the works of these eminent men have one capital defect. They entirely ignore the Christian doctrine of free justification from the guilt of all past sin through faith in the sacrificial blood of Christ. They all undertake the hopeless task of grafting the various graces of the Christian character upon the corrupt stock of human nature, and make no provision whatever for removing the stains of guilt from the conscience. Kempis, of course, as a Romish monk, held that men are justified by their personal conformity to the moral law of God. Bishop Taylor held substantially the same view. He was a man of a devout spirit ; the most eloquent divine that England ever bred ; a man of profound and varied scholarship ; a high Churchman ; but an unsound theologian. On the subject of original sin he embraced the semi-Pelagian theory; and his sermon entitled *Fides Formata* is an elaborate attempt to refute the doctrine of justification by faith only : a doctrine to which, as a clergyman and a prelate, he had oftener than once declared his assent and consent.

William Law, on the subject of a sinner's justification before God, departed still further from the truth. It does not, indeed, appear from any part of his writings that he had a distinct apprehension of justification, in the forensic sense, and especially of the justification of "the ungodly." He acknowledged that the death of Christ was a sacrifice for sin, but not a propitiatory sacrifice; for as he denied that there is any wrath or anger in God on account of sin, there could be no need of a propitiation. There was no wrath to appease, no anger to avert. His principles, when pushed to their logical consequences, lead to a denial of future punishment in the case of those who die in their sins, as Mr. Wesley proved at a subsequent period of his life. Christ as a Teacher, and as an Example, Law distinctly acknowledges, but is silent on the subject of our Lord's priesthood. In his writings, beautiful as they often are, we look in vain for just and scriptural views of Christ as the Mediator between God and men, and as a Saviour from sin. Whether Mr. Wesley ever entertained Law's entire theories is uncertain; but we have his own acknowledgment, that when he went to Georgia, and during his residence there, he confounded justification with sanctification; and gave himself no

serious concern about the forgiveness of his sins;
thinking that this blessing would in an unknown
manner come upon him in the hour of death or in
the day of judgment. * It is indeed strange that so
sensible and thoughtful a man should have expected
forgiveness only at the close of life, or even at the
end of time, inasmuch as all believers are described
in the New Testament as living in the present
enjoyment of that inestimable blessing.

While he remained in this state of mind, his
views of faith were not only defective, but even
erroneous.† He thought that faith is nothing more
than simple belief; the assent of the mind to the
truths of the Gospel; not adverting to the fact,
that thus far the devils believe, and that millions of
mankind yield such an assent, and yet live and die
in their sins. Whereas true faith, "the faith of
God's elect," is inseparably connected with salvation
both from sin and its penalty. Justifying faith is
the gift of God. He reveals Christ as the object of
faith; He gives the authority and warrant to trust
in Christ for salvation; He imparts the power to
believe in Him; He stimulates and urges men to
the exercise of that power. Faith is a coming to
Christ, a looking unto Jesus; a trust, a confidence
in Him, a reliance upon Him; and the man who
thus comes, believes, and trusts, does so for the
express purpose of obtaining forgiveness. "We
have believed in Christ, that we might be justified

* Wesley's Works, vol. viii., p. 111.   † *Ibid.*

by the faith of Christ," is the declaration of an apostle. (Gal. ii. 16.) In other words, justification is the benefit which the believer desires and expects to receive, when he comes to the Saviour. Nor must it be forgotten, that where faith is, there is union with Christ. Christ dwells in the believer, and the believer is in Christ. As the members are one with the head in the human body, and as the branches are one with the vine, so are believers one with Christ; and faith is the bond of their union. Faith is not a mere mental assent, but an appropriating act. Christ hath "loved *me*," says the apostle, and " gave Himself for *me*." (Gal. ii. 20.)

It was not only in respect of justification, and of the faith by which that blessing is received by individual men, that Mr. Wesley's judgment was at fault in the early years of his ministry. His views concerning the operations of the Holy Spirit were also defective. To attain to a state of entire sanctification was with him the great business of life; he aimed at a high standard of personal holiness; but in the process of this work his references to the grace of the Holy Spirit were rather casual and indirect, than indicative of an entire dependence upon His presence and agency. He rather regarded the mortification of sin in his nature as the result of personal effort and self-denial, than as the direct effect of the Holy Spirit's power. He expected to possess the mind that was in Christ, not as an immediate communication from above, but rather as the consequence of fasting, of prayer, of self-denial, and the constant repression within him of every unholy feeling. Yet, after all, he made little or no progress; inward sin still held him in bondage; and hence his subsequent solution of his case :—

> " Too strong I was to conquer sin,
>   When 'gainst it first I turn'd my face;
> Nor felt my want of power within,
>   Nor knew the' omnipotence of Grace.
>
> " In nature's strength I sought in vain
>   For what my God refused to give:
> I could not then the mastery gain,
>   Nor lord of all my passions live."

He apprehended not the proper import of the prayer which his lips daily uttered, " Make clean our hearts within us; " and knew not that he could never be made free from " the law of sin and death," but by " the law of the Spirit of life which is in Christ Jesus." He did not rightly apprehend the promise, " A new heart also will I give you; " nor the declaration of John respecting Christ, " He shall baptize you with the Holy Ghost, and with fire."

The truth is, the men whom he had chosen as his guides caused him to err. He was orthodox. He believed every article of the three Creeds as sincerely as did St. Athanasius himself; but he was far from rightly apprehending the office of Christ as

D

the Redeemer and Saviour of men, and the office of
the Holy Ghost as their Comforter and Sanctifier.
A writer in the "London Quarterly Review" for
January, 1868, says, "We have before us a number
of unpublished sermons written by John Wesley, at
Oxford, during the ten years which followed his
ordination....In not one of them is there any view
whatever, any glimpse, afforded of Christ in any of
His offices. His name occurs in the benediction.
That is about all. Frequent communion is insisted
on as a source of spiritual quickening; regeneration
by baptism is assumed as the true doctrine of the
Church; but Christ is nowhere, either in His life,
His death, or His intercession. Church formalism
and strict morality, ceremonies and ethics, are all
in all." A brighter day, however, at length dawned
upon him.

The history of the Church presents many
examples of providential arrangement and interposition, which ought to be observed and devoutly
acknowledged; and the meeting of two men at the
period of which we are now speaking was far from
being casual, or a matter of mere chance. One of
them was an anxious inquirer after truth, and the
other was eminently qualified to impart it. At the
very time when Mr. Wesley in America, harassed
by persecution, and perplexed as to the state of his
mind and heart, resolved to return to his native
land, the heads of the Moravian Church in Germany
were making arrangements for sending one of their

pious and gifted evangelists to America, resolving that he should pass through England, and pay special visits to London and Oxford; little imagining what momentous consequences would arise from the fulfilment of their plans. The hand of God was in the whole affair. The man selected for this service was Peter Böhler, who arrived in London just in time to impart the evangelical instruction which Mr. Wesley and his brother Charles so greatly needed, and were prepared to receive.

Mr. Charles Wesley had returned to England a few months before his brother, with whose religious opinions and feelings he had an entire sympathy. Both of them being in the same state of mind and heart, Böhler's counsel was as applicable to the one as to the other. He was introduced to them both, not together, but successively; and we may safely say that when they met, little time was spent on either side in observations concerning the weather, European politics, or unimportant disputes among literary men. The Wesleys, long perplexed and anxious, wanted to know what they must do to be saved from sin, to be made holy, and permanently happy in God. The devout German, full of holy zeal, at once saw their condition, and administered appropriate counsel, not deduced from any school of philosophy, but from the Scriptures of truth. We can easily conceive of John Wesley as saying in the fulness of his heart, " I have spent twelve or thirteen years in attempts to attain to a state of inward purity, and, after all, have made no progress ; being yet carnal, and sold under sin.

> " ' Where is the way? Ah, show me where,
> That I Thy mercy may declare,
> The power that sets me free :
> How can I my destruction shun ?
> How can I from my nature run ?,
> Answer, O God, for me ! ' "

The language appropriate to Böhler was,—

> " My heart is full of Christ, and longs
> Its glorious matter to declare."

The substance of what he advanced was this :— Man is a sinner, depraved and guilty. Christ died as a propitiatory sacrifice for sin, and is a Saviour from it. The salvation of which He is the Author is a free gift. It is bestowed without money and without price, and is received by faith on the part of sinners. Faith is a simple trust in Christ; a trust of the heart; connected with repentance, in which sin is lamented, confessed, and forsaken; a trust connected also with an entire renunciation of all self-confidence. Directly consequent upon the exercise of faith on the part of a penitent sinner is an application of the Saviour's blood, purging the conscience from dead works; so that guilty terrors cease ; peace and joy spring up in the heart; for the Holy Spirit bears " witness " to the spirit of the believer that he is an adopted child of God, and therefore an heir of glory. "The fruit of the Spirit" directly follows His witness : and that fruit is "love, joy, peace, longsuffering, gentleness, goodness, faith, meekness, temperance." (Gal. v. 22, 23.) The believer in Christ, therefore, being made free from the guilt and curse of sin, is invested by the Holy Spirit with the Christian character, and is prepared to serve the Lord in "newness of life," being at once both happy and holy.

This doctrine appeared strange to the Wesleys, who had previously entertained no distinct apprehension of a sinner's justification before God, and who had considered mental and bodily suffering as the grand means of mortifying inward sin, from which they only expected complete freedom by death. To the doctrine of which they now heard for the first time they offered many objections, chiefly derived from the mystical philosophy in the meshes of which they had long been entangled. In reply, Böhler appealed to the Holy Scriptures, the teaching of which every man is bound to receive in the spirit of a little child; reminding them that their vain philosophy must be purged away, so as to give place to "the truth as it is in Jesus." After consulting the oracles of God, the brothers yielded their assent to the teaching of Böhler, especially when they heard it confirmed by the testimony of other persons; for the Wesleys were not the only men to whom the pious German offered present freedom from the guilt and misery of sin through faith in the blood of the cross. Others heard, believed, and found rest unto their souls.

Having fulfilled his brief mission in England, Böhler embarked for America, leaving the Wesleys hungering and thirsting for the righteousness of faith. In a very short time Charles found peace with God, as he lay on the bed of sickness in the house of a brazier in Little Britain, near Smithfield; and, a few days after, John obtained the same blessing at a religious meeting close by in Aldersgate-street, while listening to Luther's Preface to the Epistle to the Romans, containing a description of the change which takes place in a man's state and feeling when he believes in Christ with the heart unto righteousness.

Being now possessed of the true key to all sound religious experience, and of a power in their ministry which they had never wielded before, the brothers immediately entered upon an energetic course of evangelical labour, calling sinners to repentance, and proclaiming to rich and poor, old and young, men and women of moral habits, and profligate transgressors, including convicts under sentence of death, pardon and peace, as "the common salvation," to be obtained, by all alike, through faith in the blood of Christ. Others caught the theme, and carried on the work, which has been successfully prosecuted to the present day. But for "the wormwood and the gall" of which the Wesleys so bitterly tasted during the dreary years of their novitiate, they never would have fulfilled their evangelical mission with the energy and strength of resolution which characterized their subsequent labours. To the end of his life Charles Wesley used to say that William Law was their John the Baptist; and much did they suffer while they knew nothing beyond his baptism. Mighty was their deliverance and their joy when Peter Böhler "taught them the way of God more perfectly."

It is worthy of special observation, that St. Paul, who declares the Gospel to be "the power of God unto salvation," declares it to be such especially because it embodies the doctrine of present justification through faith in Christ crucified. His words are, "I am not ashamed of the Gospel of Christ: for it is the power of God unto salvation to every one that believeth; to the Jew first, and also to the Greek. FOR therein is the righteousness of God revealed from faith to faith." (Rom. i. 16, 17.) The attempt to relieve the consciences of guilty men by any other means is perfectly useless and unavailing; and the attempt to subdue their evil propensities and habits by their own efforts, without the sanctifying Spirit, is as useless as to tell "the Ethiopian to change his skin, and the leopard his spots." But when the guilt of sin is taken away, and the Holy Spirit assumes the possession of the heart, "old things are passed away, and all things become new." If any man could by himself attain to happiness, and to purity of heart, John Wesley

would have succeeded; but even he, after the labour
of thirteen years, found that he was still the slave
of sin, and made this humiliating confession:—

> " My mouth was stopp'd, and shame
> Cover'd my guilty face ;
> I fell on the atoning Lamb,
> And I was saved by grace. "

No scheme of religion meets the wants of a
sinful world, unless it contains a provision for the
forgiveness of all past sin, and the investiture of
sinners with the privileges of righteousness. This
the Gospel does; and hence its " power " in restor-
ing men to happiness and to moral purity.

To be taught the nature and the appointed method
of justification before God was not the only benefit
received by Mr. Wesley from his interviews with
Peter Böhler. His attention was then effectually
called from such speculatists in religion as William
Law, to the oracles of God; and from that time
he became " a man of one book," subjecting every
doctrine to the test of Holy Scripture. Hence his
abandonment of everything in the form of philoso-
phical speculation in matters of religion, and the
thoroughly evangelical character of his future
labours both in the pulpit and in the use of the
press. Up to this period he had published little;
but from this time, as he generally occupied the
pulpit daily, so he kept the press continually
employed to the end of his life. In addition to a

large number of cheap volumes and pamphlets which he published, he gave the world his views of religion, experimental and practical, in a series of sermons, which for clearness of exposition and force of argument have never been surpassed by any other writer in the English language; declaring, at the same time, his absolute deference to the authority of the Bible, and the spirit in which he studied it.

" I have thought," says he, " I am a creature of a day, passing through life as an arrow through the air. I am a spirit come from God, and returning to God : just hovering over the great gulf; till, a few moments hence, I am no more seen ; I drop into an unchangeable eternity ! I want to know one thing,— the way to heaven ; how to land safe on that happy shore. God Himself has condescended to teach the way ; for this very end He came from heaven. He hath written it down in a book. O, give me that book ! At any price, give me the Book of God ! I have it. Here is knowledge enough for me. Let me be *homo unius libri.** Here, then, I am, far from the busy ways of men. I sit down alone. Only God is here. In His presence I open, I read His Book ; for this end, to find the way to heaven. Is there a doubt concerning the meaning of what I read ? Does any-thing appear dark or intricate ? I lift up my heart to the Father of Lights : Lord, is it not Thy word,

* " A man of one book."

'If any man lack wisdom, let him ask of God?' Thou 'givest liberally, and upbraidest not.' Thou hast said, 'If any be willing to do Thy will, he shall know.' I am willing to do, let me know, Thy will. I then search after and consider parallel passages of Scripture, 'comparing spiritual things with spiritual.' I meditate thereon with all the attention and earnestness of which my mind is capable. If any doubt still remains, I consult those who are experienced in the things of God; and then the writings whereby, being dead, they yet speak. And what I thus learn, that I teach." *

After Mr. Wesley had received the truth, and found rest to his soul, he addressed a letter of remonstrance to William Law, complaining that he had never directed his attention to the Gospel method of justification before God. We conceive that it was right in him to make this complaint, considering the authority which Mr. Law had invariably assumed on religious subjects; yet the blame did not rest exclusively with the mystic philosopher. Mr. Wesley was also a clergyman, and ought to have been a more diligent student of the New Testament, and of the formularies of his own Church. He would not then have leaned so entirely upon the broken reed which pierced his hand, and left him to be healed by a man of greater skill, with a more tender heart.

* Preface to his Sermons.

The change in Mr. Charles Wesley was as strongly marked as that in his brother. As the pensive disciple of William Law, he could claim no assured interest in the benefits of the Saviour's sacrifice, and therefore only muttered in a low and subdued tone,—

> " Doubtful and insecure of bliss,
> Since death alone confirms me His :
> Till then to sorrow born, I sigh. "

But after he had received the truth in the love of it, he thus poured forth the joyous feelings of his soul :—

> " My God, I am thine, What a comfort Divine,
> What a blessing to know that my Jesus is mine !
> In the heavenly Lamb Thrice happy I am,
> And my heart it doth dance at the sound of His name. "

In the same triumphant strain he poured forth his feelings in glorious hymns, till his spirit returned to God.

" Behold, how great a matter a little fire kindleth !" The announcement of the simple element of Gospel truth, present justification by faith in Christ,—not as a theory, but as matter of personal experience, with other concomitant doctrines,—led to the forma- tion of the Wesleyan-Methodist Connexion, with its numerous offshoots both at home and abroad ; to the Methodist Episcopal Church in America ; and to a large number of foreign Missions in every quarter of the globe ; to say nothing of the Episcopal clergy- men and the Dissenting ministers whom Methodism has supplied within the last hundred years. Such are the results of the few brief and godly interviews which took place between a Moravian Missionary and the two Wesleys in the year 1738. "Who hath despised the day of small things?" How many thousands and tens of thousands of people, in England and in far-distant lands, since the time of Böhler's visit to London and Oxford, have obtained the faith and salvation which he recommended to the Wesleys, and have died in the joyful hope of being for ever with the Lord! To God be all the glory!

A modern writer has asserted, with an air of authority, that the mission of the Wesleys differed from the mission of Luther; that of Luther being the revival of the doctrine of justification by faith, and that of the Wesleys the revival of the doctrine of the new birth. We enter our protest against this idle distinction. The mission of the two parties was identical. The Wesleys acknowledged no new birth but that which is consequent upon justification, and is inseparably connected with it; and they acknowledged no justification from the guilt of past transgression but that which is obtained by faith in the blood of Christ. They did preach the new birth with earnestness and fidelity; but their first concern was to make their hearers sensible of their guilt, and bring them in a penitent state of heart to Christ, that through His death and intercession they might receive the blessing of full and free forgiveness. The Wesleys were impressively taught by their own experience, that until men are personally justified, there is no hope that they will be either regenerated, or built up in holiness. The justifying faith which they taught is effectually guarded against antinomian abuses by the fact that it is always preceded and accompanied by true repentance, and is followed by purity of heart and a holy life. Where these adjuncts are wanting, there is neither true faith, nor justification, nor the new birth. Hitherto the men who have entered into the labours of the Wesleys have " walked according to the same rule ; " and to the end of the world it is hoped they will " mind the same thing."

Within the last few years certain periodical works, conducted by Ritualistic clergymen, have expressed great respect for Mr. Wesley, and the writers have claimed him as belonging to their brotherhood, chiefly on the ground of his sayings and doings in Georgia, and before he entered upon his mission there. He then held the theory of apostolical succession ; refused to administer the Lord's Supper to a Dissenter, unless he would submit to be rebaptized ; and turned his face to the east when he repeated the Creed. He most probably mixed the sacramental wine with water ; prayed standing on Whit-Sunday ; and certainly deemed himself a sacrificing priest. We would suggest to the gentlemen who admire John Wesley on account of these things, that a distinction should be drawn between John Wesley the Ritualist, the ascetic disciple of William Law, and John Wesley the converted evangelist; just as a distinction should be made between Saul of Tarsus, and " Paul an apostle of Jesus Christ by the will of God." As a Ritualist and a disciple of William Law, Mr. Wesley was unhappy; his preaching was powerless, and of very little use to mankind. When he had " put off the old man," and was invested with a truly evangelical character, he was heartily ashamed of his former deeds; he possessed a " peace which passeth all understanding," and was one of the most useful men that ever lived. In reference to his ritualistic and ascetic follies, he was ever ready to say, " When I was a child, I spake as a child, I understood as a child, I thought (reasoned) as a child : but when I became a man, I put away childish things." The sooner his ritualistic admirers follow his example, the better it will be for themselves, their congregations, and the country at large.

Of late years much has been said on the subject of " succession " in the Christian Church. One of the ablest men among the Episcopal divines of the seventeenth century (George Lawson) said that personal succession was of very little moment, unless it were connected with a succession of sound evangelical doctrine. From the facts which are now before the reader of these pages, it appears that the Wesleyan Methodists are in a succession of which they have no reason to be ashamed. They have received their general orthodoxy from the Church of England, through the medium of Mr. Wesley, as the founder of their Societies. They received their doctrine of justification by faith, as matter of personal experience, from the Moravian Church, an honoured and venerable community, which claims descent from the Bohemian Brethren, including the noble confessors, John Huss and Jerome of Prague.* Nor should it be forgotten, that it was while listening to the words of Martin Luther that John Wesley himself obtained the faith and salvation of the Gospel. These are interesting facts, and will be matter of gratifying thought to persons belonging to the Wesleyan body. Yet every one will do well to remember, whatever may be his ecclesiastical relationships, that there will be no admission into the society of the blessed above without personal repentance; personal faith in Christ crucified; personal justification through the shedding of His blood; personal sanctification to God in body, soul, and spirit; personal subjection to Christ's authority and will; and perseverance in all to the end of life.

* See "Report from the Committee [of the House of Commons] to whom the Petition of the Deputies of the United Moravian Churches in behalf of themselves and their United Brethren was referred: together with Extracts of the most material Vouchers and Papers contained in the Appendix to the said Report. 1749." This is a folio volume of one hundred and fifty-six pages, and contains a very interesting record of the history, tenets, and economy of the Moravian Brethren.

The body of Wesleyan Methodists, and Christians in general who take an interest in the spread of true religion, are greatly obliged to Mr. Lockwood for the pains he has taken in collecting information concerning the personal history of Peter Böhler, and arranging it in the narrative which is now before the reader. He has supplied intelligence which many persons have desired to possess, but knew not where to find it. Respecting Mary of Bethany our Saviour said, that wherever His Gospel should be preached, her pious act in anointing His feet should " be told for a memorial of. her ; " and we may now say that whenever the origin of genuine Methodism is investigated, the character and services of the man from whom the two Wesleys received the counsel which led to their spiritual emancipation, and to the truly evangelical character of their ministry, will not be forgotten. " The memory of the just is blessed."

MEMORIALS OF PETER BÖHLER.

CHAPTER I.

THE following Memorials present the religious character of a minister and bishop of the Moravian Church, or the Church of the United Brethren, which claims to be regarded as the oldest Protestant organization; and whose members refer with honest pride to their descent from the Church founded in the mountains of Bohemia in 1457,—a Church which has recorded in its martyrology the names of Jerome of Prague and John Huss, and which has recently celebrated its fourth centenary.

The Council of Constance, which was opened on November 5th, 1414, and continued until April 22d, 1418, possessed no common significance. How intense must have been the excitement of the age which assembled twenty-nine cardinals, three patriarchs, thirty-three archbishops, one hundred and fifty bishops, more than one hundred abbots, a still larger number of theological professors and doctors, more than five hundred monks, and a mis-

E

cellaneous gathering of more than fifty thousand persons, from the Emperor downwards! Pope John XIII., who entered with a splendid retinue, in which one thousand six hundred horses were counted, was deposed, and escaped in the disguise of a groom; Gregory XII. and Benedict XIII. were also superseded. How exciting must have been the discussions of that stirring period! And how eventful the four centuries which have elapsed since Huss and Jerome were burnt at the stake, and their ashes thrown into the Rhine!

The renewed Church of the Brethren dates from the foundation of Herrnhut on June 17th, 1722; and in August, 1732, the infant community, then numbering about six hundred members, first essayed to fulfil the final charge of our ascending Lord by sending out its messengers to the distant nations of the earth.

A host of honoured names cluster about the events of 1722, of which Zinzendorf forms the central figure. Zinzendorf and Böhler are inseparably associated: between the two a most sacred vow was made, that they would be true to the cause and service of their common Lord even to the death.

From Zinzendorf Böhler received episcopal ordination; and, under his direction, he shortly afterwards undertook a mission to America, his official instructions comprising a visit to Oxford. It was this visit which, under God, led to the conversion of John and Charles Wesley, and to the commencement of the great revival which, having exerted an ever-growing influence for a century and a quarter, is, we devoutly trust, intended to bless all evangelical churches, and to hasten the final triumph of the Saviour's kingdom.

With interest akin to that with which we trace a noble river to its source, or revisit a scene rendered classic by patriotic or religious associations, we would recall names which will never die, and review events whose importance it is difficult to exaggerate.

Frankfort-on-the-Main is a pleasant city, remarkable for its literary institutions and its historic interest. At the close of the eighth century Charlemagne built a palace in which a Council of the Church was held. Beneath its " Römer " the election of the Emperors of Germany was partly conducted ; and in its vicinity they afterwards received the homage and acclamations of their subjects. Its archives contain many valuable manuscripts ; and, among others, the celebrated Golden Bull, promulgated by Charles IV., in 1356, and written on forty-five skins of parchment. Fine specimens of mediæval architecture still linger in its principal buildings. Here the Rothschilds commenced their financial operations; and though its half-yearly fairs are not what they were in the sixteenth century, when forty thousand persons were wont to assemble within its walls, they still present a scene of great interest and extensive business.

E 2

Here, a few hours before the bells of its cathedral rang the funeral-knell of 1712, our future bishop, Petrus Böhler,* was born. He was the fourth child of John Conrad Böhler and his wife Antonetta Elizabetha Hanf, who were married April 26th, 1706. The sacrament of baptism being almost invariably administered on the third day after birth, young Peter was baptized January 3d, 1713.

Of the elder Böhler few records are preserved. In the municipal archives of Frankfort we find that "John Conrad Böhler, brewer, son of a burgher, took the oath December 22d, 1705, and paid burgher-money six florins;" and in the protocol of the Town-Council of 1736 (folio 89, B) the following entry occurs:—"John Conrad Böhler, burgher, comptroller at the Corn-Office." Dr. Konig, who has kindly conducted extensive inquiries, adds, "The office of comptroller to the Government bureau was often given to persons who, though unsuccessful in business, were otherwise well qualified for a trust so important." His position was respectable; and at his house the Founder of Methodism found a hospitable reception, when a pilgrim bent on no common errand.

"On Monday, July 3d, 1738," writes Wesley, "at half an hour past ten, we came to Frankfort. Faint and weary as we were, we could have no admittance here, having brought no passes with us;

* Pronounced Bäyler.

which, indeed, we never imagined would have been required in a time of settled, general peace. After waiting an hour at the gates, we procured a messenger, whom we sent to Mr. Böhler; (Peter Böhler's father;) who immediately came, procured us entrance into the city, and entertained us in the most friendly manner." For the details of Wesley's conversations at Herrnhut, we must refer to his Journals, as they are too voluminous and important to admit of condensation. In the return-journey he remarks: "Monday," (August) "28th, I took my leave of the Countess; (the Count being gone to Jena;) and, setting out early the next morning, came about three in the afternoon to Frankfort. From Mr. Böhler's we went to the Society, where one of the brethren from Marienborn offered free redemption through the blood of Christ to sixty or seventy persons."

Of the other branches of the burgher's family our notices are very scanty. Several of the three sons and six daughters with which their union was blessed died in their youth. The oldest child was baptized May 22d, 1707; and the youngest, October 15th, 1726. We find the name of Francis Böhler, who was born in 1722, went to Bethlehem in 1753, and, after serving as minister in several of the Brethren's churches, died January 4th, 1806, at Lititz, in Pennsylvania. Böhler's letters speak of a sister, most probably Salome Böhler, who came from Ebersdorf to reside at Gnadenthal; and was, we imagine, the lady who married Brother Gerner, and died December 9th, 1764. The name of William Böhler also appears in the diary of the Church.

Young Peter early exhibited great aptitude in the acquisition of knowledge. Beginning to attend school at four years of age, he commenced the study of the Latin tongue at eight, and entered the following year the Gymnasium of his native city, then under the rectorship of John Thomas Klump. The following entry in its Album thus notes his admission :—" No. 55, 1722, d. 28 (September), Peter Böhler, of Frankfort-on-the-Main, aged nine years. Placed in class VI."

The worthy burgher had intended his son for the medical profession, in which he might, doubtless, have won renown and acquired wealth ; but his rapid advances in learning, and his eminent abilities, led to the selection of a theological training,—a decision fraught with the most important results.

Böhler's boyhood, though not unchecked by the monitions of conscience, nor destitute of vigorous efforts after a purer morality, was wild and wicked ; but, at this most critical period of life, an event occurred which, by the good providence of God, led him to religious decision, and proved the commencement of a career of eminent spirituality and usefulness. He accompanied a clergyman of the city to visit a woman under sentence of death for an attempted murder, who expressed in most touching terms her deep abhorrence of the fearful crime she

had contemplated; but also affirmed her full conviction that her sins were pardoned by an application
of the Saviour's blood. The truth thus presented
in strains so impressive, and under circumstances so
solemn, found a prompt response in the breast of
young Böhler. Restraining his emotion while
within the condemned cell, he retired hastily to his
own room, and sought relief to his feelings in fervent prayer and abundance of tears. He now entered
on the hopeless task of self-reformation, and his
experience amply sustains the teaching of Divine
truth, that, until the fountain is made pure, the
streams will be turbid and polluting. "Can the
Ethiopian change his skin, or the leopard his spots?
then may ye also do good that are accustomed to do
evil." Böhler's experience proves most conclusively,
that evangelical obedience can only spring from a
regenerate heart. His intense solicitude for the
Divine favour became almost overwhelming, and his
mental anguish bordered upon despair. In this
frame of mind, after delivering a valedictory address
in Latin, he bade adieu to the beautiful city of his
birth, and proceeded to the University of Jena.

This celebrated University was founded by the
Elector John Frederick, who, in passing through the
Grand Duchy of Saxe-Weimar, as a prisoner of the
Emperor Charles V., advised his three sons to make
Jena the nurse of the sciences, and the preserver of
the true Protestant faith, instead of Wittenberg, of
which he had been deprived.

Böhler's associates at Frankfort were not helpful to him, either in intellectual pursuits, or the discipline of the heart. He speaks of them as " his gormandizing, tippling, and fighting countrymen,"— terms which reveal the perils by which his path had been beset, and show how narrow was his escape from a complete wreck of character, and from utter ruin.

Several members of the roystering band having been recently transferred to Jena, his spiritual danger was extreme. Happily, Baumeister, a pious student, afterwards a bishop, who had come to Jena a few days before the arrival of his friend, was so disgusted with the state of morals, that he had sought refuge with the " Brethren ; " and when Böhler reached the post-house, at one in the morning, he found Baumeister in attendance, to conduct him to the house of Mr. Walch, where their religious meetings were held. Böhler, without any definite purpose, followed him to the place ; and when in the early morning he was assailed by the importunities of the godless party, who besought him to leave the persecuted pietists, he was deaf to their entreaties and their taunts, and felt as though restrained by an invisible hand.

The following day he was formally entered on the University Album in the following terms:—" Petrus Boehler, Mœno-Francofurtiensis, d. 21 mensis Aprilis, ann. 1731, in numerum civium academicorum Jenæ receptus." The very first week of his

residence at Jena was memorable, not only as the
commencement of his University curriculum, but
especially as the beginning of a new spiritual life.
On April 25th he attended a meeting held by
Spangenberg, then a professor in the University, in
the lecture-hall of Dr. Walch, (successively professor
of elocution, poetry, and theology, and the author
of many valuable works, and who died in 1775,) in
which he commented on a pamphlet of Spener's. A
sentence expressive of the Saviour's power to free from
all sin caught the ear of Böhler.   The effect was instantaneous. "I have tried everything in the world
excepting this," exclaimed the conscience-stricken
student; "but this I will try!" Retiring to the
house of the pious Deacon Brumhardt, where he
had secured lodgings, and found a welcome retreat
from the scoffs and profanity of the witlings and
sceptics who unhappily abounded, he resolved
to seek the blessing of forgiveness in the evangelical
mode of which Spangenberg had been the faithful
expositor. After combating a perilous temptation
to procrastinate, he, on the following Saturday, cast
himself, in the spirit of genuine penitence, at the
Saviour's feet; and, while engaged in secret prayer,
he was enabled to believe upon the Son of God, and
immediately realized the peace and joy he had so
long and so earnestly desired. Most fitly might his
feelings have found expression in the inspiring strains
of his English tutor:—

" We who in Christ believe,
    That He for us hath died,
We all His unknown peace receive,
    And feel His blood applied ;
Exults our rising soul,
    Disburden'd of her load,
And swells unutterably full
    Of glory and of God."

The witness of the Holy Spirit to his personal adoption, thus distinctly realized, was well-nigh lost through the indiscretion of his Jena friends, who plied him with pamphlets and treatises ; but, selecting the Holy Scriptures, and especially the New Testament, as the staple of his reading, and cultivating a devout and humble spirit, he was preserved amidst numerous temptations, and, being established in the faith, became " valiant for the truth."

Böhler's conversion produced its legitimate results. He now regarded the Christian ministry, not as an honourable profession, or an arena for the exhibition of literary eminence or rhetorical skill, but as a sacred charge, for which each candidate should possess the special call of the Head of the Church, and the peculiar mental and spiritual fitness which the Lord the Spirit can alone supply. He prosecuted his studies with the zeal of a " soul in its earliest love." Intensely desirous to spread the sweet savour of Christ, he became an occasional teacher in the primary school at Jena, where his labours were greatly blessed ; several of his pupils subsequently obtaining a "good degree" in the Moravian Church. Meanwhile, good Deacon Brumhardt had exchanged the militant for the triumphant church, and the devoted Spangenberg had been transferred to the University at Halle. From various causes the number of the associated students had been reduced to nine; and at their request Zinzendorf appeared, to re-organize the little band.

It was during the visit of the Count to Jena in 1732, that the life-long attachment between him and Böhler was formed. Their intercourse was greatly blessed, and passages like the following might be freely quoted from the manuscripts of the youthful student:—
"The year 1733 was an increasingly happy one for me, and was spent in constant intercourse with the Saviour: the foundation of my future usefulness was then laid."

During the Christmas celebration of the preceding year he had preached his first sermon, and at a small village near Jena he commenced the ministry which was so eminently and extensively blessed of the Lord.

At the request of his parents, he revisited the city of his birth. The three years which had elapsed since he left it, like the stricken deer to weep apart, had been eventful ones; and he now returned an established and devoted Christian, "filled with all joy and peace in believing." His conversation, counsels, and prayers were so greatly blessed, that his father, mother, and, it is believed, every member of the family, became fully decided for God. While we regret that no record of their spiritual career can be discovered, we trust that they have met as an unbroken household before the heavenly throne.

By the direction of his father he now entered the University of Leipzig, where the official record, as certified by Dr. Boettger, states that "Peter Böhler, from Frankfort-on-the-Main, matriculated at Leipzig on June 16th, 1734, under the rectorship of Professor John Erhard Kapp, had already been entered at Jena in the year 1731." His residence at Leipzig was but brief, as, from causes which do not appear, he shortly returned to Jena. Here his influence in promoting spiritual good was extensive and powerful. The little band of nine increased to one hundred; of whom more than half joined the Moravian Church. Many of these reappear as evangelists and pastors in distant lands, and are doubtless sharing with him in the honours and rewards of the heavenly state.

On recovering from an attack of low fever, he paid his first visit to Herrnhut; and, while preaching "with a warm and melted heart," Schulius, with whom we shall meet in South Carolina, was led to the Saviour. When the "banished Count" had to bow to an unrighteous sentence, Böhler procured lodgings for his suite in Frankfort, and the Ronneburg was ultimately purchased as their residence.

Having been released from liability to military service, he now became " Magister legens," and thus obtained the right to lecture as a junior professor. His appointment by Count Zinzendorf to be the English tutor to his son occasioned great excitement in the academic senate, and in the courts of the reigning princes of the Grand Duchies; but he passed through the searching inquiries instituted by the literary and national authorities with unstained honour and perfect success.

He was doubtless anticipating the future with the buoyant hopes of an enthusiastic student, and the chastened spirit of one who had placed himself entirely at the disposal of his covenant Lord, when, on September 4th, the young Count and John Nitschman appeared as the bearers to him of a call to become the pastor of the infant church at Savannah, and an evangelist to the Negro population of the district. "A man's heart deviseth his way; but the Lord directeth his steps." Great must have been the contrast between the academic groves of Jena and the inhospitable climate of Georgia; between an attached circle of alumni at the University, and the sable sons of Ham, or the aborigines of North America, proverbially treacherous, malevolent, and cruel. But Böhler " conferred not with flesh and blood;" the vows of Jehovah were upon him: regarding the call of the Head of the Church as altogether irrespective of country, or race, or dialect, he accepted it in its full extent; for the solemn covenant into which he had entered con-

tained the clause, "even to the death." He would
not, indeed, have shrunk from the sacrifice, even
though it had been certain that he would be numbered among the multitude beheld by the disciple
whom Jesus loved, as he saw "under the altar the
souls of them that were slain for the word of God,
and for the testimony which they held: and they
cried with a loud voice, saying, How long, O Lord,
holy and true, dost thou not avenge our blood on
them that dwell upon the earth?" To that "noble
army" how many faithful witnesses have since been
added! To the call of Christ and His Church
Böhler promptly responded. Taking leave of his
Jena friends in a lovefeast held on the 13th, and
attended by many to whom he had been the instru-
ment of salvation, and followed by their prayers
and tears, he commenced on the following day the
journey to Herrnhut, where, on the 23d, he was
formally received into the Brethren's Church. Having officiated as a Lutheran minister in the parish
of Berthelsdorf until relieved by the arrival of
Mücke, he proceeded to the Ronneburg; and in the
private chapel of the old feudal fortress, where the
robbers of the Middle Ages had planned their ma-
rauding expeditions, and divided their ill-gotten
spoil, and where nobles had held their court with
princely splendour, he was solemnly ordained on
December 16th, by Zinzendorf and Bishop Nitschman, as a minister of the Moravian Church. He then
received his official instructions, which included

directions to visit Oxford on the way to his distant sphere of toil.

Thus He who " led His people like a flock by the hand of Moses and Aaron," and Himself preceded them in the pillar of a cloud by day, and the pillar of fire by night, conducted His servant to those scenes of usefulness which we purpose to review, and prepared him for labours which terminated only with his life.

CHAPTER II.

AMID the stirring scenes of the metropolis, few localities are more suggestive to a Methodist minister than the vicinity of St. Paul's. Almost beneath the shadow of that venerable cathedral are Aldersgate-street, where, as the burden dropped from his weary spirit, John Wesley found his heart "strangely warmed;" Little Britain, where, at the house of Bray, the brazier, Charles Wesley found the pearl of great price; and the old, dingy chapel in Fetterlane, which is supposed to date its erection from the days of Charles II., and, after being sacked and gutted in the Sacheverell riots, and narrowly escaping a similar fate in the "No Popery" riots of Lord George Gordon, became the centre of Moravian operations. This chapel was also the scene of the remarkable lovefeast held on the first day of the year 1739, and attended by both the Wesleys, together with Hall, Kinchin, Whitefield, Hutchins, and some sixty other brethren, when, "about three in the morning," says Wesley, "as we were continuing instant in prayer, the power of God came mightily upon us, insomuch that many cried out for exceeding joy, and many fell to the ground. As soon as we were recovered a

little from that awe and amazement at the presence
of His majesty, we broke out with one voice, ' We
praise Thee, O God : we acknowledge Thee to be the
Lord.' "

Not very distant is the place where the first interview between Böhler and Wesley occurred. Böhler
had proceeded to the house of Mr. Weynanz, (or
Weinantz,) a Dutch merchant; and on the day of
his arrival John Wesley delivered to him a letter
addressed to Zinzendorf, from John Töltschig, a
Moravian minister, whose acquaintance Wesley had
formed in Georgia. Between Böhler and Wesley an
ardent attachment at once sprang up; and the latter
hastened to procure lodgings for his friend at Westminster, near to Mr. Hutton's, where he was himself
residing.

Wesley had just returned from his Georgian
mission,—a mission which, after being the occasion
of much personal discomfort, had proved a mournful failure. Its story, as related by himself, would
furnish a " Tract for the Times " now passing over the
Christian Church, and be suggestive of truths of
deepest significance and permanent value. It would
show how a clergyman of blameless morality and
high principle, an accomplished classical scholar,
a skilful logician, and a strict observer of the rubrics
and canons of the Established Church, had failed to
apprehend the spiritual nature of evangelical religion, and was a stranger to its saving power. His
sincerity was unquestionable ; his devotion to duty

r

was beyond all praise; but he had not yet come, as undone and helpless, to rest on Christ alone for salvation, and to seek a *gratuitous* justification through His perfect sacrifice. In some most striking passages, quoted in the " Introduction " to this narrative, he tells us how the melancholy conviction now forced itself upon his mind, that he who had gone to America to convert others was himself destitute of that great spiritual change which the New Testament describes as essential to Christ's people.

But, having reached this conclusion, the mind of Wesley was graciously prepared for juster views of the Christian salvation than those presented by the writers who had hitherto been his religious guides.

That the instructions of Böhler should include a visit to Oxford must be ascribed to a higher source than mere human sagacity; and we gratefully recognise the guidance of "Him who holdeth the seven stars in His right hand," who has made the spiritual interests of His church the object of His ceaseless care, and whose prerogative it is to select, prepare, and bless the agents employed for its revival and prosperity.

The history of the conversion of the Wesleys is before the world; but as the connexion of Böhler with that event is not so extensively known, a few notices from his private papers may not be unacceptable; while brief extracts from the Journals of the two brothers may help to present a consecutive narrative of that important event.

What transpired between the 6th and 17th of February, 1738, is at best matter of conjecture; but on the latter day the two brothers and their German friend proceeded by coach to Oxford, (a journey not so expeditiously performed as in the present day, since Antony a Wood was two days in accomplishing it by the mail-coach,) and were entertained by Mr. Sarney, an old friend of the Wesleys.

Here their character and engagements soon provoked the mirth of the godless students then collected on the banks of the Isis. The reproach which they had formerly endured now revived; and even as they walked through the squares of the colleges, they became the occasion of derisive laughter. Upon one of these occasions, Böhler, perceiving that Wesley was troubled chiefly for his sake, said, with a smile, "*Mi frater, non adhæret vestibus:*" "My brother, it does not even stick to our clothes."

During the journey Böhler's mind had been painfully exercised. That he, a foreigner, who could only speak in broken English, should presume to become the instructer of the members of colleges venerable as the abodes of learning, and favoured with the prelections of some of the most accomplished professors of the age, became the occasion of severe mental conflict; but the tokens of the Divine favour were so abundant, and the disposition of the more serious students to profit by his private counsels became so marked and encouraging, that his

Journal of that period breathes the spirit of gratitude
and joy.

"February 17," writes Charles Wesley, "I came
in the Oxford coach to my old lodgings at Mr.
Sarney's." "All this time," observes John Wesley,
"I conversed much with Peter Böhler; but I understood him not, and least of all when he said, ' *Mi
frater, mi frater, excoquenda est ista tua philosophia :* '
' My brother, my brother, that philosophy of yours
must be purged away.' " On the 20th he began to
receive English lessons from Charles Wesley; and on
the 22d he pressed on the students the necessity of
more intimate union in meetings analogous to the
Methodist class-meeting.

Böhler's impressions shall be given in his own
words :—"I travelled with the two brothers, John
and Charles Wesley, from London to Oxford.*
The elder, John, is a good-natured man. He knew
that he did not properly believe in the Saviour, and
was willing to be taught. His brother, with whom
you [Zinzendorf] often conversed a year ago in
London, is at present very much distressed in his
mind, but does not know how he shall begin to be
acquainted with the Saviour. Our mode of believing
in the Saviour is so easy to Englishmen that they

* Some apparent discrepancies in dates are reconciled by
the fact that Böhler employed the new style, and Wesley the
old. The reader must pardon the rugged paragraphs, as, even
at the sacrifice of elegance, the idioms of Böhler are scrupu-
lously preserved.

cannot reconcile themselves to it : if it were a little more artful, they would sooner find their way into it.......Of faith in Jesus they have no other idea than men generally entertain. They justify themselves ; therefore they always take it for granted that they believe already, and would prove their faith by their works ; and thus so plague and torment themselves that they are at heart very miserable."

How gladly would we reproduce their earnest conversation, as they threaded the quadrangles of the colleges, or enjoyed their quiet evening walk in their vicinity ! But regrets are unavailing. Doubtless, the nature of true faith, the faith by means of which the penitent sinner receives justification, and which is followed by the assurance of the Divine favour,—that faith which Böhler had exercised in his private room at Jena, but which the Wesleys had yet to put forth,—formed the central topic of discourse, and furnished the absorbing, if not the exclusive, theme of earnest intercourse.

How attractive Böhler's conversation proved we may infer from the extensive influence he acquired, not only at Jena, but also at Oxford. One illustration of this—by no means a solitary one—may suffice. Escorted by a graduate, he proceeded to examine the University library, probably the splendid Bodleian collection ; and after spending half-an-hour amidst its literary treasures, he addressed his learned companion in the Latin tongue, and kept him spellbound for two hours, as he discoursed on "the

Lamb of God which taketh away the sin of the world."

John Wesley's visit to Oxford was brief. Returning to London on the 20th, he preached the following day at Great St. Helen's; and, after an audience with the Georgia trustees, he preached on the following Sabbath in three of the London churches; observing characteristically, "I believe it pleased God to bless the first sermon most, because it gave most offence; being indeed an open defiance of that mystery of iniquity which the world calls 'prudence,' grounded on those words of St. Paul to the Galatians, 'As many as desire to make a fair show in the flesh, they constrain you to be circumcised; only lest they should suffer persecution for the cross of Christ.'"

On the following day he took the coach for Salisbury, saw his widowed mother, and probably Mr. and Mrs. Hall, with whom she now resided; and was preparing for a visit to his brother Samuel at Tiverton, when intelligence of the expected death of Charles at Oxford led him to hasten to his room. John Wesley was a rigid economist of time; and amid the anxieties of such a journey he found opportunity to renew and transcribe his former resolutions. "1. To use absolute openness and unreserve with all I should converse with. 2. To labour after continual seriousness, not willingly indulging myself in any the least levity of behaviour, or in laughter; no, not for a moment. 3. To speak no word which does not tend to the glory of God; in particular, not to talk

of worldly things. Others may, nay, must. But
what is that to thee? 4. To take no pleasure
which does not tend to the glory of God; thanking
God every moment for all I do take, and therefore
rejecting every sort and degree of it which I feel I
cannot so thank Him in and for."

Ere we enter the sick-chamber of Charles, we
must recall an incident or two. He was doubtless a
fellow-passenger with John in the Oxford coach on
February 17th; and on the following Lord's day
received the sacrament once more at Christ Church.
How suggestive and affecting must have been the
associations of that day! Charles's Journal records the
fact of close conversation with his German pupil, who
enforced the necessity of more intimate union among
the awakened, by referring to the case of many who
had fallen asleep again for the want of it:—a moni-
tory circumstance which may well awaken solemn
thought in the minds of all whom it may concern.
Böhler was hastily summoned to his presence, and
promptly responded to the call. "Charles Wesley,"
he remarks, "has been very ill during the last
night; therefore he sent for me at break of day, and
begged I would pray for him, for the health of his
soul and body. Soon after he fell asleep the pain
became less severe. He acknowledges that these
sufferings came from God, as well as the relief
which he now experiences."

The interview is recorded in the Journal of
Böhler's friend. "At eleven," writes Charles, "I

waked in extreme pain, which I thought would quickly separate soul and body. Soon after, Peter Böhler came to my bedside. I asked him to pray for me : he seemed unwilling at first, but, beginning very faintly, he raised his voice by degrees, and prayed for my recovery with strange confidence. Then he took me by the hand, and calmly said, ' You will not die now.' I thought within myself, ' I cannot hold out in this pain until morning. If it abates before, I believe I may recover.' He asked me, ' Do you hope to be saved ? ' ' Yes ! ' ' For what reason do you hope it ? ' ' Because I have used my best endeavours to serve God.' He shook his head, and said no more. I thought him very uncharitable, saying in my heart, ' What, are not my endeavours a sufficient ground of hope ? Would he rob me of my endeavours ? I have nothing else to trust to.' "

The following night was spent by Böhler in Wesley's room, where the nature of their intercourse can only be inferred, as no memoranda have been preserved. How earnest must have been the conversation, and how fervent the supplications presented under circumstances so critical ! At Charles Wesley's request, Böhler communicated with him when, on the following day, the sacrament of the Lord's Supper was administered by Gambold ; and Böhler again kept vigil by his friend, who was not considered out of danger.

This illness of the future bard of Methodism was very severe, and had well-nigh proved fatal. He was thrice bled; and they poured down draughts, oils, and apozems without end: but the balance now inclined towards recovery; his invaluable life was spared; and the prayer of Böhler was destined to receive a more signal accomplishment.

Events of deep significance now follow each other in rapid succession. John Wesley had reached the lodgings of his afflicted brother on Saturday, March 4th. "I found my brother," he writes, "at Oxford, recovering from his pleurisy; and with him Peter Böhler; by whom, in the hands of the great God, I was on Sunday, the 5th, clearly convinced of unbelief, of the want of that faith whereby alone we can be saved."

From Böhler's manuscripts we learn that the event so fraught with future blessings occurred during a quiet evening walk. "I took a walk with the elder Wesley, and asked him about his spiritual state. He told me that he sometimes felt certain of his salvation, but sometimes he had many doubts; that he could only say this, 'If what stands in the Bible be true, then I am saved.' Thereupon I spoke with him very fully; and earnestly besought him to go to the opened fountain, and not to mar the efficacy of free grace by his unbelief. I also consulted with him about the inquirers at Oxford, and made several proposals having in view their growth in knowledge and grace. Later in the evening Wesley and other students met, and we had a religious conversation. The case of a prisoner who had been

condemned to death gave me occasion to speak of
the duty of seeking souls for the Saviour." "Immediately," adds Wesley, "it struck into my mind,
'Leave off preaching. How can you preach to others,
who have not faith yourself?' I asked Böhler
whether he thought I should leave it off or not. He
answered, 'By no means!' I asked, 'But what can
I preach?' He said, 'Preach faith till you have it;
and then, because you have it, you will preach
faith.'"

Böhler's visit had extended to three weeks,
and most unsparingly had he scattered the seed of
which the harvest was to be so rich and abundant.
He gratefully records the fact, that, in addition to
his success in the University, more than a hundred
citizens of that ancient city were under religious
awakening. He now returned to London, John
Wesley contributing six shillings towards his
travelling expenses.

Another journey to Oxford becoming necessary,
he had the opportunity of renewing his unostenta-
tious labours, of which "the most remarkable
feature," observes Böhler, "was a very full conversation which I had with the two Wesleys, in order
to impress upon their minds the Gospel, and in
order to entreat them to proclaim the same to
others, as they had opportunity, at Oxford and
elsewhere. Thereupon they confessed their doubts
respecting the truth of the doctrine of free grace,
through the merits of Jesus, whereby poor sinners

receive forgiveness, and are set free from the dominion of sin. The Saviour, however, granted me grace to convince them from the Scriptures; and they had no way of escape, except to ask to see and converse with persons who had made the experiences of which I spoke. I told them that in London I hoped to be able to show them such Christians."

John Wesley remarks, "I met Peter Böhler again, who amazed me more and more by the account he gave of the fruits of living faith,—the holiness and happiness which he affirmed to attend it. The next morning I began the Greek Testament again, resolving to abide by 'the law and the testimony,' and being confident that God would thereby show me whether this doctrine was of God."

On Saturday, April 22d, another interview occurred; and the Journals of Wesley and the Böhler manuscripts are again mutually illustrative and suggestive. "I met Peter Böhler once more," writes Wesley. "I had now no objection to what he said of the nature of faith; namely, that it is (to use the words of our Church) 'a sure trust and confidence which a man hath, that through the merits of Christ his sins are forgiven, and he reconciled to the favour of God.' Neither could I deny either the happiness or holiness which he described as fruits of this living faith. 'The Spirit itself beareth witness with our spirit that we are the children of God,' and, 'He that believeth hath the witness in himself,' fully convinced me of the former; as, 'Whosoever is born of God doth not commit sin,' and, 'Whosoever believeth is born of God,' did of the latter. But I could not comprehend what he spoke of an instantaneous work. I could not understand how this faith should be given in a moment; how a man could at once be thus turned from darkness to light, from sin and misery to righteousness and joy in the Holy Ghost. I searched the Scriptures again, touching this very thing, particularly the Acts of the Apostles; but, to my utter astonishment, found scarce any instances there of other than instantaneous conversions; scarce any so slow as that of St. Paul, who was three days in the pangs of the new birth. I had but one retreat left; namely, 'Thus, I grant, God wrought in the first ages of Christianity; but the times are changed. What reason have I to believe He works in the same manner now?' But on Sunday, the 23d, I was beat out of this retreat too, by the concurring evidence of several living witnesses; who testified God had thus wrought in themselves; giving them in a moment such a faith in the blood of His Son, as translated them out of darkness into light, out of sin and fear into holiness and happiness. Here ended my disputing. I could only cry out, 'Lord, help Thou my unbelief!'"

"I took," says Böhler, "four of my English brethren to John Wesley,......that they might relate their experience to him, how the Saviour so soon and so mightily has compassion, and accepts the sinner. They told, one after another, what had been wrought in them; Wolff, especially, in whom the change was quite recent, spoke very heartily, mightily, and in confidence of his faith. John Wesley and those that were with him were as if thunderstruck at these narrations. I asked John Wesley what he then believed. He said, four examples were not enough to prove the thing. To satisfy his objections, I replied, I would bring eight more here in London. After a short time he stood up, and said, 'We will sing that Hymn, *Hier legt mein Sinn sich vor dir nieder.*' " *

> " My soul before Thee prostrate lies,
> To Thee, her Source, my spirit flies,
> My wants I mourn, my chains I see :
> O, let Thy presence set me free !

> " Lost and undone, for aid I cry ;
> In Thy death, Saviour, let me die !
> Grieved with Thy grief, pain'd with Thy pain,
> Ne'er may I feel self-love again.

> " Jesu, vouchsafe my heart and will
> With Thy meek lowliness to fill ;
> No more her power let Nature boast,
> But in Thy will let mine be lost.

* " The original was composed by Dr. Christian Frederick Richter, a pious physician, well read in theology, and connected with the Orphan-House at Halle at the time of the celebrated A. H. Francke. He, along with his brother, prepared the drugs which were known as the 'medicines of Halle,' and, being in great repute, tended not a little to defray the expenses of the institution." The above version is that of Wesley, 1739.

" In life's short day let me yet more
Of Thy enlivening power implore :
My mind must deeper sink in Thee,
My foot stand firm, from wandering free.

" Ye sons of men, here nought avails
Your strength ; here all your wisdom fails :
Who bids a sinful heart be clean ?
Thou only, Lord, Supreme of men.

" And well I know Thy tender love ;
Thou never didst unfaithful prove :
And well I know Thou stand'st by me,
Pleased from myself to set me free.

" Still will I watch, and labour still
To banish every thought of ill ;
Till Thou in Thy good time appear,
And sav'st me from the fowler's snare.

" Already springing hope I feel ;
God will destroy the power of hell ;
God from the land of wars and pain
Leads me where peace and safety reign.

" One only care my soul shall know,—
Father, all Thy commands to do :
Ah ! deep engrave it on my breast,
That I in Thee even now am blest.

" When my warm'd thoughts I fix on Thee,
And plunge me in Thy mercy's sea,
Then even on me Thy face shall shine,
And quicken this dead heart of mine.

" So even in storms my zeal shall grow ;
So shall I Thy hid sweetness know ;
And feel (what endless age shall prove)
That Thou, my Lord, my God, art love."

"During the singing of the Moravian version," Böhler continues, "he often wiped his eyes. Immediately after he took me alone into his own room, and declared, 'that he was now satisfied of what I said of faith, and he would not question any more about it; that he was clearly convinced of the want of it: but how could he help himself, and how could he obtain such faith? He was a man that had not sinned so grossly as other people.' I replied that it was sin enough that he did not believe on the Saviour: he should not depart from the door of the Saviour until He helped him. I was very much pressed to pray with him: therefore I called upon the bleeding name of the Saviour to have compassion on this sinner......Afterwards he told me what contradictions he had met with from the pious clergy with whom he had taken counsel, because he had by opportunity told them what he knew, and what he still wanted; but he was not concerned at it. He asked me, moreover, what he should do at this time, whether he should tell all the people his present state or not? I replied that in this I could give him no rule; that he might do what the Saviour would teach him; that he must not set the faith as it is in Jesus so far from him, but believe that it might be nearer; that Jesus's heart still stands open, and that His mercy towards him is great. He wept heartily and bitterly, as I spoke to him on this matter, and (insisted that) I must pray with him. I can say of him, he is truly a poor sinner, and has a contrite heart, hungering after a better righteousness than that which he has till now possessed, even the righteousness of Jesus Christ.

"In the evening he preached from 1 Cor. i. 23: 'But we preach Christ crucified, unto the Jews a stumbling-block,' &c. He had above four thousand hearers, and spoke upon this subject until the congregation was astonished, because no one had ever heard such things from him. His first words were, 'I hold myself from my very heart unworthy to preach the crucified Jesus.' All poor sinners can describe it; yes, all who remain convinced of their wretchedness. There have been many awakened by it."

The most persevering researches have hitherto failed to discover contemporary notices of an event so unusual. Imagination must call up the associations of that hour:—the deep emotions of the clergyman now for the first time proclaiming truths so novel, yet so solemn; the tender pathos of his earliest attempt to stir the human heart to its utmost depths; the varied impressions produced on more than four thousand hearers; and the "many awakenings" which furnished an appropriate sequel, and proved the first-fruits of a glorious harvest, to be gathered from every land, and through all succeeding periods of time. What suggestive subjects for devout meditation! What a scene for the pencil of the artist!

Wesley returned to Oxford on the 26th, Böhler walking with him a few miles; but he was hastily recalled by tidings of his brother's relapse,...... which had led to great searchings of heart. "Having disappointed God in His last visitation," observes Charles, "He has now again brought me to the bed of sickness. Towards midnight I received some relief by bleeding. In the morning Dr. Cockburn came to me, and a better physician, Peter Böhler, whom God had detained in England for my good. He stood by my bedside, and prayed over me, that now, at least, I might see the Divine intention in this and my late illness. I immediately thought it might be that I should again consider Böhler's doctrine of faith; examine myself whether I was in the faith; and, if I was not, never cease seeking and longing after it till I attained it."

On Thursday, May 4th, Böhler left London, in order to embark for Carolina. From Southampton he wrote to John Wesley as follows :—

"IN AGRIS SOUTHAMPTONIANIS,
"*Die 8vo Maii*, 1738.

"I LOVE you greatly, and think much of you in my journey, wishing and praying that the tender mercies of Jesus Christ the crucified, whose bowels were moved towards you more than six thousand years ago, may be manifested to your soul; that you may taste and then see how exceedingly the Son of God loved you, and loves you still; and that so you

G

may continually trust in Him, and feel His life in yourself. Beware of the sin of unbelief; and if you have not conquered it yet, see that you conquer it this very day, through the blood of Jesus Christ.

"Delay not, I beseech you, to believe in your Jesus Christ; but so put Him in mind of His promises to poor sinners, that He may not be able to refrain from doing for you what He hath done for so many others. O, how great, how inexpressible, how unexhausted is His love! Surely He is now ready to help; and nothing can offend Him but our unbelief.

"Believe, therefore. Greet in my name your brother Charles and Hall; and admonish one another to believe, and then walk circumspectly in the sight of God, to fight lawfully against the devil and the world, and to crucify and to tread all sin under your feet, as far as you are permitted, through the grace of the Second Adam, whose life exceeds the death of the first Adam, and whose grace far surpasses the corruption and damnation of the first Adam.

"The Lord bless you! Abide in faith, love, teaching, the communion of saints; and, briefly, in all which we have in the New Testament.

"I am

"Your unworthy brother,

"PETER BÖHLER."

Charles's recovery was gratefully commemorated

in a hymn which presents a graphic portrait of his spiritual position. The original poem has seventeen stanzas. Among those not in the Hymn-Book are the following :—

> " My feeble flesh refused to bear
> Its strong redoubled agonies;
> When Mercy heard my speechless prayer,
> And saw me faintly gasp for ease.

> " Jesus to my deliverance flew,
> When sunk in mortal pangs I lay;
> Pale Death his ancient Conqueror knew,
> And trembled, and ungrasp'd his prey.

> " The fever turn'd its backward course,
> Arrested by almighty Power;
> Sudden expired its fiery force,
> And anguish gnaw'd my side no more."

Charles was now an inmate in the house of Bray, the brazier in Little Britain, whom he regarded as specially sent of God to supply the place of Böhler. His enfeebled health occasioned much solicitude, and on the eve of Whit-Sunday John spent the night with him. The day of deliverance was at hand. His brother went to one of the London churches to hear Dr. John Heylin preach ; and, the curate having been taken ill during the service, he afterwards assisted the Doctor in the administration of the Lord's Supper. " On leaving the church," he adds, " I received the surprising news that my brother had found rest to his soul. His bodily strength returned also from that hour. 'Who is so great a God as our God?'"

The mode of his deliverance shows that the feeblest instruments, when employed by God, can accomplish the most important results. "A plain, illiterate woman had a deep and solemn conviction that she ought to address the weeping and afflicted penitent; but, remembering that he was a scholar and a clergyman, she felt afraid to do it; and with difficulty prevailed upon herself to stand upon the stairs and say, 'In the name of Jesus of Nazareth, arise and believe, and thou shalt be healed of all thine infirmities.' He mentally replied, 'O that Christ would but thus speak to me!' and shortly afterwards was enabled to believe with the heart unto righteousness."

On the following Wednesday John Wesley " went, very unwillingly, to a society in Aldersgate-street, where one was reading Luther's Preface to the Epistle to the Romans. About a quarter to nine," he says, " while he was describing the change which God works in the heart through faith in Christ, I felt my heart strangely warmed. I felt I did trust in Christ, in Christ alone, for salvation; and an assurance was given me that He had taken away *my sins*, even *mine*, and saved me from the law of sin and death." "Towards ten," observes Charles, " my brother was brought in in triumph by a troop of our friends, and declared, ' *I believe!* ' We sang the hymn with great joy." *

* " The hymn " was, doubtless, the one composed by Charles

Both the brothers had now obtained the direct witness of the Holy Spirit, attesting their adoption into the family of God.; and their views of Divine truth began to acquire that definite form which is embodied in the doctrinal standards and the psalmody of the Church which bears their name. If apostolic purity,' fidelity, and 'love; if disinterested philanthropy and untiring zeal; if churches founded by their labours, and nurtured by their care, until they now form one of the largest Protestant communities in the world, may be regarded as furnishing any criteria of the reality of the change which the Wesleys then experienced, and the extent of the mission to which they were called ; surely we must acknowledge in these events the working of Divine grace. While we gratefully recognise the honoured names we now recall, we devoutly say, " *To God alone be immortal praise!*" Well might Wesley exclaim, "O what a work hath God begun since his [Böhler's] coming into England! such an one as shall never come to an end, till heaven and earth pass away!"

two days before, on the occasion of his own deliverance, being probably either the thirtieth or the two-hundred-and-first of the Wesleyan Collection.

CHAPTER III.

THE parting charge of the ascending Saviour, as
He addressed His disciples on the grassy slopes of
Mount Olivet, " Ye shall be witnesses unto Me both
in Jerusalem, and in all Judæa, and in Samaria, and
unto the uttermost part of the earth,"—an injunction
which will retain its unimpaired authority until the
final consummation of all things,—was not unheeded
by the Church of the " United Brethren."

When numbering about six hundred persons,
most of them poor and destitute exiles, this feeble
band of heroic men sent out, during the short period
of nine or ten years, missionaries to Greenland, to
St. Thomas, to St. Croix, to Surinam, to Berbice, to
the Indians of North America, to the Negroes of
South Carolina, to Lapland, to Tartary, to Algiers,
to Guinea, to the Cape of Good Hope, and to the
island of Ceylon.

The settlements they formed were not intended
for personal gain, nor for the acquisition of cor-
porate wealth and possessions, but to enable them
to prosecute with increased efficiency the spiritual
work in which they were so zealously engaged. They

thus furnished a refuge for the persecuted converts, and a training-school for the infant churches; while, in their physical beauty, their civilizing tendency, and especially in their spiritual results, they became as "a fruitful field, and a place which the Lord hath blessed."

Georgia, to which Böhler's steps were now directed, was a colony founded by royal charter in 1732. It was intended as an outlet for a redundant population, and a refuge for the Protestants who were compelled to flee from the unrighteous persecution of Papal governments.

Of these the city of Salzburg, and the adjacent valley, in South Germany, furnished no inconsiderable number; and it is computed, on careful estimate, that from the different European countries "not fewer than twenty-six thousand six hundred and seventy-eight persons, men, women, and children,—the aged, the sick, new-born infants with their mothers,—were driven in mid-winter from the land of their fathers, and sent forth, through fields of snow, in quest of a people who were not hardened into fiends by Papal superstition, and among whom they might live in safety and peace." *

* The merciless edict, dated October 31st, 1731, was sent forth in the name of Leopold, by the grace of God, Archbishop of Salzburg, and Legate of the Holy See Apostolical, and Primate of Germany, and addressed to "all our Vice-Deans, Bailiffs, Provosts, Governors, their substitutes, Judges, and to all our other officers."

Their migrations called forth, in the various countries through which they passed, the deepest sympathy with their sufferings, and the most profound admiration of their moral courage and fidelity; while their meek and patient demeanour under their cruel wrongs was beyond all praise. The Protestant spirit of England was stirred to its very depths, and for their relief British charity raised the noble sum of thirty-three thousand pounds.

A detachment of this noble band, of whom the world was not worthy, under the charge of Baron von Reck, and their pastors, John Martin Bolzius, and Israel Christian Gronau, were welcomed by Oglethorpe on the American strand with generous sympathy and timely aid.

The site of their first settlement was promptly selected. With their Bibles in their hands, they marked out the place, and sang a hymn, after which the pastor pronounced a benediction, and the name "Ebenezer" was given to it. No pompous procession or martial display marked the events of that interesting day. Kneeling down by the river-side, they thanked God for having brought them through so many dangers to a land of rivers and fountains of water, a land of valleys and hills. The scene almost unconsciously recalls the faith of the patriarch, who, "when he was called to go out into a place which he should after receive for an inheritance, obeyed; and he went out, not knowing whither he went;" and associates them with the ancient worthies who "confessed that they were strangers and pilgrims on the earth."

The earlier interviews of the native chiefs with Oglethorpe gave auguries of pacific and happy intercourse; and their national councils, where the questions arising from the appearance of "the pale-faced strangers" in their midst were discussed, presented specimens of effective native eloquence.

Tomo Chachi, in his first set speech, presented Oglethorpe with a buffalo's skin, bearing the painted head and feathers of an eagle. "The eagle," he said, "signified swiftness, and the buffalo strength:" —the one represented the force of flight with which the English came over the waters, and the other their might on the shore, which nothing could withstand:— "the soft feathers were a sign of love, and the warm fur was an emblem of protection; and these he hoped the English would always extend to his small and helpless people." The bearing of the native chiefs was manly and dignified. When, on one of them presenting himself to the Governor, he was told that he might speak freely and without fear, he answered, "I always speak freely; why should I fear? I am now in the presence of my friends; and I have never feared, even among my enemies."

Several chiefs accompanied Oglethorpe subsequently to England, and were presented to the King, George II., and the Queen. "This day, Thursday, the first of August, 1734," says a contemporary serial, "at one o'clock, Sir Clement Cotterel, attended by three of His Majesty's coaches, with six horses each, came to the Trustees' office for Georgia, in Old Palace-yard, and proceeded from thence, with the Indian king, queen, and chiefs, and the interpreter, to Kensington Palace, where His Majesty received them on his throne, in the presence-chamber; and Tomo Chachi, Mico or King of Yamacraw, made the following speech:—

"' This day I see the majesty of your face, the greatness of your house, and the number of your people. I am come for the good of the whole nation called the Creeks, to renew the peace which long ago they had with the English. I am come over in my old days; though I cannot live to see any advantage to myself, I am come for the good of the children of all the nations of the Upper and Lower Creeks, that they may be instructed in the knowledge of the English. These are the feathers of the eagle, which is the swiftest of the birds, and who flieth all round our nations. These feathers are a sign of peace in our land, and have been carried from town to town there; and we have brought them over to leave with you, O great King, as a sign of everlasting peace. O great King, whatsoever words you shall say unto me, I will tell them faithfully to all the kings of the Creek nations.'

" To which His Majesty gave this answer: 'I am glad of this opportunity of assuring you of my regard for the people from whom you come, and am extremely well pleased with the assurances you have brought me from them, and accept very graciously this present as an indication of their good disposition to me and my people. I shall always be ready to cultivate a good correspondence between them and my own subjects, and shall be glad of any occasion to show you a mark of my peculiar friendship and esteem.'

"To the Queen, Tomo Chachi made the following speech :—' I am glad to see this day, and to have the opportunity of seeing the mother of this great people. As our people are joined with Your Majesty's, we do humbly hope to find you the common mother and protectress of us and all our children.' To which Her Majesty returned a gracious answer.

"On August 17th they waited upon His Grace the Archbishop of Canterbury, at Lambeth ; who received them with the utmost kindness, and expressed his fatherly concern for the ignorance they were in with respect to Christianity, his strong desire for their instruction, and great satisfaction at the door being now opened towards it. His Grace, notwithstanding his present weakness, would stand up : the Mico, perceiving it to be uneasy to him, insisted upon his sitting down, which His Grace excusing, the Mico omitted speaking what he intended, and only desired his blessing ; acquainting him, that what he had further to say he would speak to the Rev. Dr. Lynch, the archbishop's son-in-law ; and then withdrew.

" He had a conference with the Rev. Dr. Lynch,
and expressed his satisfaction at the venerable
appearance of His Grace, and the tenderness he
expressed towards him. After the Mico returned,
he showed great joy, believing some good persons
would be sent to instruct their youth."

Oglethorpe had some difficulty in preventing the
Indian warriors appearing at court in the undress
of an American savage, and ornamented with bar-
baric art. Tomo Chachi and his Queen were, however,
presented in scarlet robes, trimmed with gold; and
he doubtless esteemed himself as every inch a king.

They visited the churches, palaces, dockyards;
witnessed the civic display of barges on the Lord
Mayor's day; and were deeply impressed with the
novelty and grandeur of the great metropolis. The
King allowed them £20 a month for their personal
expenditure, and on their return they received
presents to the extent of about £400. Prince William
presented the young Mico with a gold watch, the
latter promising to call on Jesus Christ every
morning as he examined it.

A parting glance may be permitted, ere we take
leave of Tomo, Chachi, whose name appears in the
Journal of Wesley, who evidently regarded him with
considerable interest. His last affliction was protracted; and he expired at his Indian town, near
Savannah, on October 5th, 1739. In accordance with
his request he was interred among the English: the
body was met at the bluff by General Oglethorpe,

who, accompanied by the civil authorities, accompanied it into Percival-square. Oglethorpe and Colonel Stevens were among the pall-bearers. Minute-guns were fired during the funeral procession; and at the close of the service three volleys fired over the grave by the militia, who were present on duty, announced that the Mico of Yamacraw was gathered to his fathers.

Amidst Böhler's numerous engagements in London the mission to Georgia was not forgotten. His memoranda mention an hour's confidential conversation with Oglethorpe, its benevolent founder, who, delighted to find him acquainted with the Arabic language, furnished him with a letter to " Squire Vernon," * at whose expense the Arabic version of the New Testament had been printed; with two guineas to purchase forty copies for presentation to the Negroes; as also ten English Bibles, and an allowance of one shilling per day during his detention in England.

A voyage to America was not so expeditiously accomplished in 1739 as by the fleet of splendid steamers which now conduct the traffic between the elder and the younger country. For several weeks,

* James Vernon, Esq., son of James Vernon, Secretary of State to William III. He was appointed envoy to the King of Denmark; and was spoken of, when not twenty-five years old, " as a young gentleman who hath a fine education, is master of abundance of learning, is very modest and sober." He was one of the Commissioners of Excise, and died in 1756.

even until the middle of July, the vessel beat about
the English coast; and when fairly under way,
she was obliged to make for the Madeiras, where
she anchored for ten tedious days : at length, after
a voyage of one hundred and thirty-four days, not
unprofitably spent, they reached St. Simon's, in
Georgia, when contrary winds again delayed the
passage of the sloop, as they coasted northwards
towards Savannah, which they did not reach until
October 15th.

How frequently would Böhler's thoughts, as the
ship lay becalmed on the Atlantic, or ploughed its
waves amid furious tempests, revert to the two Wesleys ! Since " the secret of the Lord is with them that
fear Him," would he be unconscious of the blessed
change which they had already experienced? or
would he have an impression that they were fulfil-
ling his prediction, that their salvation would prove
the life of many ?   And how great would be his
interest, as he traversed the scenes of their earnest
but unsuccessful labours, and heard from other lips
the story of their persecutions and perils !

The *animus* displayed towards the Wesleys
by persons whose names need not appear, was
bitterly hostile.   Their letters were intercepted, and
the espionage was so complete that the brothers
found it necessary to correspond in Greek and converse in Latin ; but from persecution so malevolent
they escaped with unspotted reputation.

It may not be irrelevant to note, that the lady

whose name appears most conspicuous was married
in eight days to another person, whose name
re-appears as a patron of horse-races, and who was
the member of a club of unenviable reputation; while the principal persecutor, who declared, "I have drawn the sword, and I will not
sheathe it until I have satisfaction," was himself
the subject of a presentment from the grand jury;
was dismissed from office on a charge of fraud
and embezzlement; was obliged to make an
assignment of his beautiful residence at Oak-
stead; was summoned to England to appear
before the Georgia Trustees, who required him to
return for the purpose of obtaining the needful
vouchers; and on the return-voyage found a watery
grave. Who can forbear the involuntary exclama-
tion, "Verily there is a God that judgeth in the
earth!"

Seiffart, the Moravian elder at Savannah, had
been the personal friend of John Wesley, and had
dissuaded him from his intention of joining the
Moravian Church; assuring him that God had given
him another calling, in which he might be more
extensively useful. When they met, old and grey-
headed, on Wesley's eightieth birthday, at Zeist, in
Holland, Wesley reminded his episcopal friend of the
advice he had given him in Georgia, and declared
that its soundness had been proved by the experience
of each succeeding day.

Böhler found Georgia in a tumult of political

excitement. The quarrel between England and Spain was rapidly tending to an open rupture. In the spirited debates which ensued in the British Parliament, young Pitt, who was designated by Walpole as " that terrible cornet of horse," gave promise of his future greatness. Many of the colonists, whose fears of personal safety were not groundless, had fled to Pennsylvania; and Böhler found a mere handful of brethren, and no slaves. Bent on the accomplishment of his mission to the sable sons of Ham, he, accompanied by Schulius, hasted to Purisburg, and was again disappointed to find scarce three Negroes in the town, and not a hundred within a circle of twelve miles. After conferring with Oglethorpe, they resolved to make Purisburg the centre of their operations, and entered on the work with the solemn purpose to " make full proof of their ministry." During the summer, Böhler was thoroughly prostrated by " a violent ague, a tumour, and a terrible cough ;" and his friends feared that his ministerial career was closed. As he was slowly recovering, his beloved Schulius, his first-born in the Gospel, and his inseparable friend, was seized with violent fever; and he had the mournful task of conducting the funeral solemnities,—himself but the shadow of his former self.

War was now formally declared with Spain ; and, other complications ensuing, Böhler and Seiffart led, with sad and bleeding hearts, the remnant of their flock, comprising but five men, one woman, and a boy, to Savannah. Meanwhile, the Rev. George White-field, who had reached Savannah on January 1st, 1740, sought the acquaintance of Böhler. Though the latter spoke freely of "his unedifying housekeeping" at the Orphan-House, and some smart doctrinal encounters took place between them, their mutual affection was conspicuous; and Böhler took part with the zealous evangelist in a service "attended by a multitude of people, who were addressed in the English and German tongues."

Whitefield, who had purchased five thousand acres of land on the forks of the Delaware for £2,200, now proposed that the Brethren should erect the Negro school on the Nazareth settlement; and, after an exploratory tour, the offer was formally accepted,—the Brethren regarding the proposal as a singularly opportune and providential one. Thus Böhler was the first messenger of the Church who penetrated the dense wilderness. Under his care the pilgrim-band commenced their journey on foot; and, despite the toils of travelling through forests where the white man had never trod, and amid con-tinued peril of their lives from the native tribes, on May 30th they reached their future home. Assem-bling under the shadow of a broad black oak, on the bark of which the initials of Böhler and Seiffart were visible so lately as 1799, they returned thanks in the fine hymns of their native land to the God of all grace for the continued tokens of His care and blessing. For the first time the solitudes of that vast forest were awoke by the song of praise, which, accompanied by the carols of countless birds, arose from grateful hearts, and ascended as incense before the throne of Him who is

"In the void waste as in the city full."

Severe as was the labour required for the erection of a building of massive stone, in a country where the Red Indian trapped his game, they addressed themselves hopefully to the task, and toiled amid their many difficulties with exemplary courage. Böhler adapted himself to his new position with his usual tact. He superintended the carpenters, and wielded the axe. He handled the saw with hearty good-will. He encouraged the workmen by his counsels and example; and conducted their daily services with great unction and power. He walked also to a distant mill to procure the necessaries of life, preached with his accustomed fervour on the Sabbath, and performed all the duties of a Christian pastor with rare fidelity. The spiritual life of the community was thus sustained; and Böhler refers to the period as a season peculiarly blessed of the Lord.

Amidst visitations so gracious, an unexpected order was received from Whitefield, requiring the Brethren to abandon the building, and leave the district where they had been so laboriously employed. Great was their perplexity on the arrival of a document so peremptory; but "they gave themselves unto prayer;" and, at the most critical period, Bishop Nitschman appeared, to request Böhler's return to Europe, where his valued services were urgently required.

After affectionate adieus to his true-hearted associates, and commendations of them to the providence and grace of God, he proceeded by the Great Falkner Bog to Philadelphia and New York, where he was called to encounter the most unrelenting hostility. The Presbyterian ministers not only preached against him, and went from house to house to warn their hearers against attending his ministry, but the Dutch pastors sent out their deacons to lay violent hands upon him; and threats of civil commotion, the pulling down of churches, and other outrages, were not wanting. For this bitter feeling no reason can be assigned. His career had been an eminently pacific one, his ministry was not controversial; but "prejudice has neither eyes nor ears," and these were not the times for the inauguration of the " Evangelical Alliance," or the cultivation of brotherly love.

He sailed in an old leaky vessel bound for Bristol, on January 29th, 1741; and, though the voyage was prosecuted in great peril, he reached the British shore in safety, after a passage of twenty-seven days. Here he found the aspect of spiritual affairs sufficiently discouraging. Calling hastily at Oxford and other towns, he reached the metropolis, where tidings of religious inquiry and awakening were specially welcome and reassuring.

After a brief sojourn he proceeded to join the
Pilgrim Congregation in Germany ; and, arriving at
Herrndyke, in Holland, on the same day with Spangenberg, he was pressed by the latter to return with
him to England. For Spangenberg's judgment he
entertained the most profound respect : deferring to
his high position, he accompanied him to London,
whence he was soon sent on a mission to Yorkshire.
Great was the contrast between the wilds of Pennsylvania and the busy, enterprising population of the
West Riding, where Böhler's ministry was exceedingly
popular, and where he usually preached twenty times
or oftener each week. His congregations were large,
amounting, on some occasions, to three or four thousand persons. The public mind had been thoroughly
aroused by the labours of the Wesleys, Whitefield,
Grimshaw, Ingham, John Nelson, and other evangelists, whose trumpet-tones had effectually disturbed
the spiritual slumbers of multitudes. Most exciting
must have been the scenes presented in the vales of
the Calder and the Aire, where the interest culmi-
nated, as he ascended their lofty hills, or occupied
their picturesque ravines, and proclaimed to listening and anxious crowds, " Behold the Lamb of God,
which taketh away the sin of the world." Visitations so gracious called forth his most vigorous
efforts, and the impression produced was extensive
and permanent.

How repeatedly have the faithful servants of Christ
had to mourn over the successful efforts of the

"enemy" to "sow tares among the wheat," while
seasons of special revival have sometimes been followed by events peculiarly trying to their faith and
love! To these observations Böhler's case presents
no exception. His return from Holland was the
subject of inquiry by Zinzendorf; and at this critical
juncture the unhappy rupture with the Wesleys
occurred. Into the merits of the controversies of
that period it is not the writer's province to enter,
nor would he attempt to adjust the balance of blame.
A careful review of the whole question shows that
considerable misapprehension existed, while the best
Moravian authorities now admit that the strictures
employed were not wholly uncalled for. Regrets
are now unavailing. It is due to Böhler to say, that
no unkind allusion to events of that period occurs in
his manuscripts, nor are materials furnished to
account for the temporary estrangement of the
Count. Böhler doubtless secured the " blessedness "
of the " peacemaker," and proved that " the fruit of
righteousness is sown in peace of them that make
peace."

The estrangement alluded to was exceedingly
brief,* and in November of the same year he accepted
the charge of a large body of German emigrants
who were expected to arrive in the early months of
1742. A little greatly-needed leisure enabled him to

---

* We append to this chapter two letters, which many years
subsequent to this date passed between Böhler and Mr.
Wesley.

revisit his native city, and recall, in the midst of an
attached family-circle, the events of a life singularly
rich in incident, and fruitful in spiritual results.

A hint having been given that his usefulness
would be promoted, and the interests of the Church
advanced, by the selection of a suitable partner; and
the object of his choice having been approved by the
Count, and also by the members of his family; he
was married, on February 20th, to Miss Elizabeth
Hobson, who proved a faithful wife and fellow-
helper in the faith. To his married life we can but
briefly refer;—suffice it to say, that it was in the
highest sense a happy one. Devotedly attached to
her husband, and accompanying him in some of his
most perilous enterprises, she also rendered invaluable services as a deaconess or eldress; and after
he had been subsequently consecrated a bishop, the
records of his episcopal visitations frequently refer to
the wisdom, discretion, and piety which appeared in
her intercourse with the female choirs of the church.
Her letters breathe the spirit of ardent devotion,
and her whole life was indicative of unreserved
dedication to the service of Christ and His church.
Among other memoranda we find the names of the
following children:—Anthony Peter, born 1743;
Christian, born 1746; Benigna, born 1748; and
Louis, born 1751. It is believed that more than one
died in infancy or youth; but it is probable that
Louis Frederic Böhler, who was received into the
Brethren's Church in 1763, and came to reside at

Bethlehem in 1784, where he died in 1815, was the son of the worthy bishop.   Mrs. Böhler survived her husband nearly six years, residing in the "Widows' House" at Fulneck, where, as "a widow indeed," and a venerated "mother in Israel," she calmly waited for the final call; and on March 20th, 1781, she rejoined her glorified husband in "the metropolis of souls," as heaven is aptly termed in Moravian phraseology.   The writer visited her grave (No. 629) in the quiet resting-place of the Moravian Church at Fulneck, in the summer of 1865, and found the inscription on her humble memorial perfectly distinct.

> " The soul hath o'ertaken her mate,
>   And caught him again in the sky;
> Advanced to her happy estate,
>   And pleasures that never shall die;
> Where glorified spirits, by sight,
>   Converse in their holy abode,
> As stars in the firmament bright,
>   And pure as the angels of God."

The following are the two letters referred to, p. 101:—

"To the Rev. Mr. John Wesley.
" Reverend Brother,
    "Your kind letter of the 5th instant came duly to hand, and I cannot forbear to acknowledge with these lines the receipt thereof in the most friendly manner.   At the same time I will take notice of

your last paragraph, and beg an answer to my question.

"You write,—

"'As to what is to come: I have no desire or design to speak of them' (the Brethren) 'at all.'

"This I very much approve; and I heartily wish, also, it may neither happen without a previous design. You add, 'Unless in their favour.' For my part, I would heartily dispense even with this. You conclude, 'I hope I shall never be constrained to do otherwise.' This is, properly, the sentence which startles me. For I cannot imagine what could constrain you to pass strictures on us, or to speak against us. For, dear brother, you have really lost sight of us for these thirty years past. You know us since that time only by hearsay, and mostly by what this or that person in his confusion has been pleased to say. Yet, perhaps, there may be some things in your mind which do not occur to me; and if they should be of such a nature as to be removable on our part, I beg you to mention them to me, and I will do all in my power to prevent them.

"Our brethren, and I also particularly, in my small sphere of acting, have all along been concerned to promote a universal love among all the children of God, and a universal esteem of all the servants of God towards one another, in all denominations who heartily co-operate to promote the knowledge of our crucified Saviour as the propitiation for our sins.

Indeed, it is one of the most grievous points for our mourning about the breaches in Zion, that we find so few heartily inclined for it. I must own that, ever since my last coming to England, this consideration has been a heart-breaking subject to me. For our dear Saviour's last will in John xv. is set aside: His command to love one another is neglected : and, consequently, the impression which the world should receive of knowing His true disciples, by their unfeigned love towards one another, is absolutely lost. And a great loss it is, which all real children of God should heartily bewail; at the same time standing by one another, through His grace, to remedy this essential defect. If this point was at any time absolutely necessary to insist upon, it is in the period wherein we now live. For we see that the wicked world, and even the infidel ecclesiastics as well as laymen in all denominations, rise in open defiance and rebellion against the Lord who has bought them with His most precious blood. Ah! how much more, then, should all who truly love our crucified Lord Jesus, and who indeed want to promote His glory, stand up in mutual support of each other, comfort, strengthen, and, where need is, set each other to rights, in love, meekness, humility, forbearance, friendliness, &c., as the Head of our most holy religion has set us a spotless example !

"Ah! if this were the case with the children of God and servants of Christ in all denominations, how would the glory, saving knowledge, and kingdom of our Lord Jesus Christ increase all over the world! Yea, thousands who are now stumbled at the controversies, backbitings, sly and satirical strictures on each other, &c., &c., would be linked into this bond of love and peace in our crucified Lord.

"Excuse this digression, my dear brother. It comes from a full heart, that is ready to overflow as soon as this subject is touched upon. I feel an inexpressible tenderness when I take a view all over the so-called Christian world. Towards the end of this or beginning of next month, I hope to go on a journey of about four or five weeks. After my return to London, not many weeks will elapse before I, God willing, shall set out for Germany; which, of course, reminds me of taking leave of you and all my friends and brethren in England,—which is not so easy a thing for me, as my heart is in the strictest union with them.

"You, my dear brother, may firmly assure yourself that my prayers for you and your Societies will continue for your prosperity in the crucified Lord Jesus Christ, who died for us, that we might be delivered from the hands of all our spiritual enemies, and serve Him all the days of our life in holiness and righteousness before Him. In whom I also am,

"Dear and reverend brother,

"Yours affectionately,

"PETER BÖHLER.

"*Nevil's-Court, February 13th, 1775.*"

" February 18*th,* 1775.

" My dear Brother,

"When I say, 'I hope I shall never be constrained to speak otherwise of them,' I do not mean that I have any expectation this will ever happen. Probably it never will. I never did speak but when I believed it was my duty to do so. And if they would calmly consider what I have spoken from March 10th, 1736, and were open to conviction, they might be such Christians as are hardly in the world besides. I have not lost sight of you yet. Indeed, I cannot, if you are ' a city set upon a hill.'

" Perhaps no one living is a greater lover of peace, or has laboured more for it, than me ; particularly among the children of God. I set out near fifty years ago with this principle, ' Whosoever doeth the will of My Father who is in heaven, the same is my brother, and sister, and mother.' But there is no one living that has been more abused for his pains, even to this day. But it is all well. By the grace of God I shall go on, following peace with all men, and loving your Brethren beyond any body of men upon earth, except the Methodists.

" Wishing you every Gospel blessing, I remain
" Your very affectionate brother,
" J. Wesley."

CHAPTER IV.

THE Moravian emigrants reached England on the 24th of February, 1742. They were temporarily accommodated in Little Wild-street, and promptly organized as a "sea congregation," with Böhler as their pastor. In the presence of three hundred persons an impressive charge was delivered by Spangenberg, in which the peculiar duties and responsibilities of their new vocation were affectionately and solemnly enforced.

Ere they left London, eight of the Brethren ascended the gallery of St. Paul's, and, in view of the extended panorama of the city, sang a hymn of intercession for its teeming population; they then proceeded to the vessel, formerly the "Catherine Snow," now the "Irene"* ("Peace"). Böhler shortly arrived, and commenced his pastoral duties by holding a lovefeast with his interesting charge.

Before their departure from Gravesend, Spangenberg conducted a valedictory service on deck. Exhorting them to remember "that all their days,

* Was the name of the tune "Irene" suggested to Wesley by this incident?

and times, and steps were numbered, that nothing could happen without the Lord's will," "though storms, and winds, and waves awaited them," as also the resistance of Satan and his host, he encouraged them by the assurance "that in their sorest trials God's help and blessing would be abundantly vouchsafed." Friendly salutations and affectionate adieus were freely interchanged, and with many tears and earnest prayers they were commended to the providence and grace of God.

The "sea congregation" now commenced their voyage, the perils of which were greatly enhanced by the war then violently raging. The Spanish privateers swept the ocean; and exciting scenes of chase, and all but miraculous deliverance, are recorded in the diary of the pilgrim-band. One of them had been impressed for service on board a man-of-war, but was promptly released. Their religious services were seasons of especial grace, and their influence on the captain and sailors was soon perceptible. "The Lord bestows great peace," writes Böhler; "nay, it is inexpressible."

Losing sight of the Kentish coast, they soon encountered a storm so severe, that they were obliged to lash the helm, and let the vessel drive before the gale. On the morning of Easter-Sunday the Brethren assembled in the early dusk, and, according to the custom of the Moravian Church, celebrated the occasion with hymns of triumphant praise. In their settlements this service is supplemented by the

Easter Litany, in which they recall the decease of
the members of the Church who have departed during the year, and unite in expressions of gratitude
and joy on their removal from the militant to the
triumphant Church.

Touching at Madeira to replenish their supplies,
they learnt with sorrow that any attempt to converse with the inhabitants on religious subjects
would expose them to the horrors of the Inquisition,
then in full operation ; but they embraced the
opportunity of addressing the priests who called
upon them, to whom, and to the inhabitants generally, their enterprise appeared a perfect riddle.

Madeira was left during a period of intense excitement, occasioned by the appearance of two suspicious foreign vessels.   Amidst the beating of
drums, the discharge of musketry, and the respon-
sive shouts of the crews on board of the men-
of-war, they sailed through the anchored fleet,
and with a prosperous breeze resumed their
voyage.

Ere long their fears were aroused by the appearance of a privateer, lightly built, to insure rapid
sailing.   She was supposed to carry from twenty to
thirty cannon, and to be manned by a crew so cruel
and barbarous, that death was considered a happier
fate than capture.   The privateer hoisted all sail,
and bore down with appalling swiftness upon the
defenceless "Irene," which had " neither powder,
nor ball, nor sword on board."

The captain, regarding seizure as inevitable, shortened sail, and calmly awaited his fate; while the Brethren, showing no fear, felt assured of the special interposition of Him to whose service they were devoted, and whose glory only they sought to promote. When they were apparently in the jaws of death, a sudden fear seemed to seize the hostile captain, who, though surrounded by his bloodthirsty crew, allowed them to pass without hindrance or molestation;—a deliverance so signal as to call forth grateful songs of praise.

Storms and tempests, thunder and lightning, mist and fog, now rendered progress all but impracticable, and often threatened the destruction of the entire party. But amidst all, their diary speaks of peculiarly blessed visitations in their religious services. In a lovefeast, held on the anniversary of Böhler's awakening, he largely referred to the circumstances of his own conversion. How valuable would have been notes of that address!

At length the western continent appeared in sight. They touched at New-Haven, where their arrival awakened great excitement among the students, who insisted on their paying a visit to the University; when they were called to reply to a pamphlet containing twenty-two points of polemic divinity. This unwelcome task being briefly closed, they preached to the students. The inhabitants listened with delight to the discourse of the Brethren who were able to speak

English. Crowds followed them on board their vessel, and remained until midnight; while the slightest intimation of a service on shore, either in a dwelling or in the open air, attracted an eager group of listeners, who "appeared to pull the word out of their mouths."

Tearing themselves away from New-Haven, they reached New-Greenwich, where they were regarded as marauders intent on plunder. But their addresses speedily disarmed hostility; and the inhabitants followed them in great numbers through the streets, to listen to their edifying converse. The party left behind at Little London were also engaged in the same pleasing task, and the Negroes were delighted to unite with them in their religious exercises; for the distinctions of colour and race have no place in the Church of our common Lord. The extent of their recent perils now became more fully apparent. They learned that at the place of their detention, not fewer than fifteen English ships had been captured by the Spaniards, while other disasters were also reported.

Their own providential preservation called forth songs of thanksgiving in unison with the inspiring stanzas of Wesley,—

> " Thine arm hath safely brought us
> A way no more expected,
> Than when Thy sheep Pass'd through the deep,
> By crystal walls protected.

Thy glory was our rear-ward,
Thine hand our lives did cover,
And we, even we, Have pass'd the sea,
And march'd triumphant over."

Proceeding to New York, where Böhler spent a day with his friends, they again put out to sea. Rounding the Cape of Delaware, they reached, after repeated dangers from lightning, tempest, and other incidents, the city of Philadelphia in safety on June 7th, 1742, while Zinzendorf (it being Ascension-Day) was preaching in one of the Lutheran churches. As soon as Divine service was closed, he hastened to the vessel, and great was their mutual joy.

The evils of slavery, then so prevalent, and which continued to fester like a gangrene on the great Republic, until it perished in the recent national convulsion, receive fresh illustration from the following extract:—" When Brother Rauch and Büttner came on board, many others came too, who thought we had been brought to be sold ; for there is a great trade carried on in this manner with white people brought for this purpose from Europe. So there was also a ship at anchor close by us full of so-called 'transports' from Ireland, who were to be sold, and who looked pitiful enough." What Christian heart does not bound with gratitude to God as he remembers that these are among the former things which have passed away ? And who would not devoutly anticipate the time,

" When the wind, as it blows o'er the ocean's bright wave,
  Shall never waft with it the sighs of a slave ?"

America, not yet severed from the mother-coun-
try, was a colony of the British Crown. Official
notice of their arrival having been given to the
Governor, they were not allowed finally to leave the
vessel until they had been presented before the
magistrates, who required them to swear that " they
would acknowledge the King of England as their
lawful sovereign, and would not oppose him ; " that
they would " conduct themselves as faithful subjects
in this country, and not take up their abode in any
other land but their own ; " and that they would
" renounce the Pope and his religion." To this the
Brethren replied that they had scruples respecting
the taking of an oath, but would give any satisfaction
that was required ; which they did by affirming in a
loud voice, sentence by sentence, as dictated by the
magistrate, the purport of the oath. The necessary
papers were then signed in duplicate, one for the
Imperial Crown, and the other for the authorities of
Pennsylvania.

Having thus fulfilled all the requirements of " the
powers that be," they were dismissed with best
wishes for their prosperity in the land of their adoption. The expenses of their voyage, amounting to
six hundred pounds, were gladly defrayed by the
Moravian Church.

The seventh Union Synod of Pennsylvania having

commenced its session shortly after their arrival, they presented a memorial for formal recognition and admission to its spiritual privileges. Böhler and three of his fellow-elders were examined on doctrinal and other questions, and their claims for admission were then endorsed.

The German emigrants proceeded at once to Bethlehem, while Böhler remained for some time with the English Brethren; and in the discharge of his duties visited the settlements at Nazareth, Bethlehem, and other places. In the fall of the year he joined Zinzendorf at Oley, and accompanied that zealous servant of Christ in his last and most perilous mission to the Indian tribes. The toils of this journey, through primeval forests, where the sound of an axe had not been heard, and through morasses requiring careful exploration, were very great. They had to cross the Susquehanna by swimming, and had no path but the circuitous and intricate hunting-track of the aborigines; thus passing through scenes of hardship and privation which it is difficult to realize. During a resi-dence of twenty days with the Shawanhose, a mur-derous plot was formed for the massacre of the entire party, which was only discovered and defeated by the special providence of Him whose sleepless eye rests with peculiar tenderness on the faithful herald of the Cross. Often were they called to "sow in tears;" but rich and abundant has been the spiritual harvest.

Böhler shortly afterwards returned to his beloved
flock at Bethlehem ; and their first celebration of the
holy Communion was long and gratefully remem-
bered as a season of inexpressible blessing. His position and talents were now fully appreciated ; and at
the eighth Pennsylvanian Synod he was chosen
Moderator, an office for which he was eminently
qualified. He now spent some time in Philadelphia,
where several Quakers had been recently baptized,
and had become members of the Church. In January, 1743, he accompanied Zinzendorf to New York,
and doubtless took part in the valedictory services,—
services which were worthy of the closing labours of
the Count on the American continent.

Böhler remained in New York several weeks.
His ministry was highly popular and greatly blessed :
even the Jews attended in numbers, to hear the
spirit-stirring addresses of the Moravian evangelist.
But bigotry and exclusiveness were in the ascendant,
and much persecution ensued. Incited by others,
the mob proceeded to acts of violence. Böhler,
being accused of being a Papist, was summoned
before the magistrates of New York, but was sen-
tenced without the opportunity of defence. His
letter to a magistrate shows that, while submitting
to an unrighteous decision, he fully understood, and
could maintain with spirit, his position as a subject
of the British Crown. That letter we subjoin :—

"January 25th, 1743.

" MAY it please your Honour :   Whereas sentence has been pronounced against me, under your Honour's authority, to the effect that I should remove from here this morning, I think myself obliged to inform you, in the first place, that I intend humbly to submit to this sentence, and to leave the city of New York before dinner-time, because I and my brethren do not choose to do anything contrary to the magistrates of any place, except the Lord of heaven and earth require it of us, in which case we fear neither death nor banishment, as we have learned to suffer persecution for Christ's sake ; and then we pray that the Lord may not lay it to their charge.

"In the second place, I think I must earnestly complain of the proceedings of the magistrates towards me ; for I have not been tried, yea, not so much as heard. No law has been alleged against me, nor any reason given for the sentence.   I presented myself for trial, but was refused ; security was promised, yet all in vain.   I am a minister of Jesus Christ, and a presbyter of the Moravian Church, which, according to the judgment of the present Archbishop of Canterbury, Dr. John Potter, is an apostolical, episcopal, orthodox Church.   It was on this account that his Grace the Archbishop recommended the whole Moravian Church to the associates of the late Rev. Dr. Bray, to commit to the said Moravian Church the conversion of the Negroes in Carolina.   Thereupon I was ordained and sent by the bishops of the Moravian Church to England, and presented to his Grace the Archbishop, who gave me his approval, and bestowed his blessing on my undertaking. General Oglethorpe took me over in one of His Majesty's transports, and recommended me [to go] to Carolina, where I stayed eighteen months, till I received a call to go to Pennsylvania. After remaining nine months there, I returned to England at the desire of my superiors. I sojourned somewhat more than a year in Europe, and then returned to these parts again. All this I can prove, and I can give security for the correctness of what I say.

" Ever since I came into the dominions of the King of Great Britain, which took place in 1738, I have proved myself a loyal subject of His Majesty King George II. and the royal family ; and this holds good not only with regard to myself, but to all my Moravian brethren. I have preached here at the request of well-known freeholders of this city, and my preaching has been exercised here publicly. I have not spoken a word whereby the Government could be offended, or any person in town. I have spoken nothing against our most holy religion, nor against good manners, as all those who have heard and understood me must own and bear witness to. My only subject has been Christ crucified for the sins of the whole world.

" Upon these premises I address myself to your Honour, hoping you will let me enjoy the same

liberty which others of my profession enjoy. Honourable Sir, I desire nothing but justice; and, in the
expectation that justice will be done me, I assure
you that I am, with submission,
"Your humble servant and unfeigned well-wisher
in Christ,
"PETER BÖHLER, *Vicar of the
Protestant Congregation of Brethren at Bethlehem.*"

The cause of this hostility cannot now be fully
explained. We do not affirm that the Moravians
were altogether blameless, or that their mode of
presenting Christian doctrine was invariably dis-
creet and wise; but there is reason to believe that
the principal cause of offence was the ancient one,
—the enmity of the carnal mind to the pure religion
of the Lord Jesus Christ.

Banished from the populous city of New York,
he once more returned to his friends at Bethlehem, and found solace and refreshment in the
discharge of his pastoral duties. In 1743 and 1744
he presided at six Union Synods, where his wisdom and piety were alike apparent. The annual
lovefeast at Philadelphia, attended by Moravians,
Germans, Swedes, Americans, Englishmen, and the
representatives of other nations, and by the members of the different evangelical churches, furnished
a pleasing contrast to scenes over which we would
gladly draw the veil of charity, and tended to the
cultivation of brotherly love. In that hallowed and

delightful service the objects of the Evangelical Alliance of the present age were anticipated; and the prayer of our Lord, that all His people "might be one," was, to a large extent, blessedly realized.

The arrival of Spangenberg, in November, 1744, released Böhler from his engagements in Pennsylvania. After visiting all the stations, he sailed from New York, at early daybreak, on April 8th, in "The Queen of Hungary." The early part of the voyage was, on the whole, expeditious and pleasant, though a careful examination of the vessel after a heavy gale revealed considerable cause for solicitude, if not alarm. As they approached so near the European continent that the colour of the water was perceptibly changed, and the lead sounded seventy-five fathoms, while meditating on a text for the next day, "Therefore I will look unto the Lord; I will wait for the God of my salvation; my God will hear me," (Micah vii. 7,) they communicated to each other their fears that danger was impending. At early dawn a suspicious sail was espied in the distance. She was shortly joined in hot pursuit by two other vessels which acted in concert; and, despite their utmost skill in lightening their vessel, and crowding sail, until "The Queen of Hungary" was greatly endangered by the rapidity of her flight, the hostile ships bore down upon them, amidst the whistling of bullets, with such fury that the captain, finding escape impracticable, at length surrendered.

The hostile crews now boarded "The Queen of Hungary," and "plundered as for a wager, quarrelling so greatly about the division of the spoil, that one party was pursued with drawn swords by the other." The Brethren bore the loss of all things, except the clothes upon their backs, with much composure, but felt concerned for the official papers and legal documents placed under their care, which were rudely trampled upon by their reckless visiters.

It was decided that the passengers should be divided among the different vessels; and seeing them hesitate to comply with this decision, the brutalized crew rushed upon them with naked swords, and drove them on deck; but, while they were bidding each other adieu with many tears and prayers, the former instructions were countermanded, and they were allowed to share each other's society. "O, how fervently," remarks the writer of the Diary, "we thanked the Lord Jesus for His great mercy!"

As they sailed under their unwelcome escort, they caught sight of the Scilly Isles, awakening longing desires to touch the shores of dear old England; and they ultimately reached St. Malo on the 5th of May. Soon after their arrival, the owner of two of the privateers, an Irishman, came on board; expressed his sincere sympathy with their misfortunes, and offered them wise counsels for their future guidance. He also secured their immunity from rigorous search, and placed their papers in the charge of a trustworthy officer.

They were now marched, two and two, through a gazing crowd, and were frequently obliged to halt from the excessive pressure. The people manifested great kindness, kissing the children, and presenting them with fruit and other things. The commissary, on learning that they were Germans, travelling to Frankfort, a neutral city, assured them of their personal liberty. Accompanied by an excited multitude, they were now conducted to the Castle, where the Governor resided, who confirmed the declaration of the commissary.

Repeated attempts to pass over to England by a flag of truce having failed, they resolved to travel by Havre-de-Grace to Holland. Friends were found who not only defrayed all present expenses, but also furnished a sufficient amount for the remaining journey.

Leaving St. Malo on May 15th, they reached Granville, where their arrival occasioned much excitement. They were requested to wait upon the Governor, whose wife, an Irish lady, sincerely pitied their condition, and promised to help them to Coutance. The sisters and children, one of them only eight months of age, being on horseback, and the brethren on foot, they advanced to St. Lo, and on the 19th entered the important town of Caen: thence they travelled near a whole day amid the shingle and stone, in the vicinity of " old ocean's

everlasting roar," in whose briny waters they were
sometimes called to wade.

Crossing the Seine to Havre-de-Grace, they again
experienced vexatious delays, and fell into the hands
of a most unreasonable and extortionary captain.
" As for the rest, it was a poor affair ; there were no
accommodations whatever. At night we were packed
together like herrings in a barrel. The cabin was
so narrow that we were obliged to lie with bended
knees, besides suffering other inconveniences ; "
which, however, were gladly borne in the pro-
spect of a speedy arrival in their beloved " Vater-
land." The remainder of the journey was quickly
performed ; and, after passing the Texel, the
towers of Rotterdam appeared in sight, and the
welcome home of Brother Leonard, whose devoted
wife, having received intimation of their approach,
had been, like our great mother,

"On hospitable thoughts intent,"

furnished a fitting reception for the weary pilgrims,
of whom the diarist quaintly remarks, that " they
had many things to tell and to be told."

From Holland Böhler proceeded to Germany,
where he resided for some time not far from the
scene of his earliest toils. Having attended the
Synod of Marienborn, from which, during its session,
his wife received her appointment as a deaconess, he
was directed in the autumn of the same year to
visit the English churches. He was also ap-

pointed the *Decanus,* or Dean, of the University of
the Brethren at Lindheim in Wetteravia.   This
appointment was opportune, and the value of his
services was fully apparent.   On the removal of the
Pilgrim Church to Zeist, and afterwards to England,
Böhler took charge of the public services at the
" Castle Church," * and in September was again
recalled to take the oversight of the English
churches.   A second sojourn at the University
was terminated by an event long expected by the
Church; and Böhler was summoned to Herrnhaag,
where, on January 10th, 1748, he was solemnly consecrated a Bishop of the Moravian Church.   The
impressive service employed in the Moravian con-
secrations is simple, and unattended by any impos-
ing ceremony.   It is opened by the singing of a
version of *Veni Creator,* a sublime hymn which
forms a fitting introduction to the sacred act.   An
appropriate discourse is delivered by the presiding
bishop, with whom one or two other bishops are
usually associated.   He also delivers a charge to the
candidate, and engages in earnest intercession for
the endowments which the Lord the Spirit can
alone supply; and then proceeds to the act of
consecration by the imposition of hands, saying, " I
consecrate thee to be a Bishop of the Church of the
United Brethren, in the name of the Father, and
of the Son, and of the Holy Ghost.   The Lord bless
thee, and keep thee; the Lord make His face to

* Query, at Marienborn or Lindheim ?

shine upon thee, and be gracious unto thee; the Lord lift up His countenance upon thee, and give thee peace. In the name of Jesus. Amen." The bishop and the congregation engage in silent prayer, and the following Doxology is sung:—

" Glory be to the *Shepherd* and *Bishop* of our souls,
  The great *Shepherd* of the sheep, through the blood of the everlasting covenant ;
  Glory and obedience be unto *God* the *Holy Ghost*, our Guide and Comforter ;
  Glory and adoration be to the *Father* of our *Lord Jesus Christ*,
  Who is the *Father* of all who are called children on earth and in heaven.
          O might each pulse thanksgiving beat,
          And every breath His praise repeat !
      Amen. Hallelujah ! Hallelujah !
          Amen. Hallelujah ! "

Wesley, who witnessed the consecration of a bishop, (probably that of good Mr. Seiffart,) at Savannah, in 1736, observes, " The great simplicity as well as solemnity of the whole almost made me forget the seventeen hundred years between, and imagine myself in one of those assemblies where form and state were not ; but Paul the tent-maker, or Peter the fisherman, presided ; yet with the demonstration of the Spirit and of power."

At the consecration of Böhler, Zinzendorf, John de Watteville, and John Nitschman were the officiating elders.

CHAPTER V.

Böhler had now received the highest honours of the Church, and efficiently and meekly did he discharge the duties of the sacred trust confided to his care. His eminent piety and fervent zeal were universally acknowledged; and are abundantly evinced by his private diary and correspondence. His attainments were more than respectable. He could expound the Psalms in Hebrew, to the delight of the sons of Abraham; he wrote a good Latin style, and conversed with ease in that language. We have seen that he was acquainted with the more difficult Arabic; and presume that he was not ignorant of Greek, as he was certainly conversant with the other languages then used by scholars, and was known at the University as "the learned Peter Böhler." His well-knit frame and robust health gave him great power of physical endurance; and, possessing a voice of great compass and melody, he often led the "service of song" in the congregations which he addressed. He was congratulated, in a short poem of fourteen verses, composed by Zinzendorf, on the forty-eighth anniversary of his birthday.

Böhler also essayed the sacred muse, but an appropriate translation of his verses is required.

His public ministry was popular and effective, and his discourses were frequently based upon the Moravian "watchword" for the day. Of these sermonic addresses copious notes have been preserved by his friends and admirers. Bishop Gambold, who was an official coadjutor, and well able to form a judicious estimate of his pulpit-abilities, remarks that "he testified searchingly;" "he delivered a very important discourse;" "he delivered a very lively address;" "he roused and moved many hearts."

As bishop, his duties were of the most onerous and varied character. Nearly all the baptisms were administered by him, evidently with great solemnity; and at the monthly administration of the Lord's Supper he presided in person, or took a prominent part in conducting that sacred service. His episcopal powers were extensive, but were exercised with admirable wisdom and discretion. They involved a visitation of the churches, including personal and minute conversation with the members, the inspection of the church property and archives, and the general supervision of its material and spiritual interests.

Böhler's appointment occurred at a most critical period. Negotiations were then in progress with the Archbishop of Canterbury, and with the Government of the day, and the parliamentary discussions were going on, which resulted in the Moravians obtaining a legal and ecclesiastical status; while the great pecuniary embarrassments which had been induced, together with the spiritual dangers which threatened, required that so long as the vessel was among the foaming breakers, its helm should be held by a firm and steady hand. Böhler's counsels were wise and Christian. The crisis was severe, and Böhler intimates that he could not have survived five additional days of similar anxiety and grief. But the hour of deliverance was at hand. A spirit less trustful might have been overwhelmed, but his mind was kept in peace; prompt and effectual aid was afforded, and the Church emerged the better and the stronger from the conflict.

On the arrival of Spangenberg, in May, 1753, Böhler consented to visit the Western Continent for the third time. After hearing from Zinzendorf an appropriate sermon on "Ye are the salt of the earth," they went on board the "Irene." The passengers, seventy-one in number, having assembled, they weighed anchor. As Plymouth, the Eddystone Lighthouse, the Lizard-Point, and the Land's-End successively disappeared, they felt that they had fairly entered upon their voyage of three thousand miles. The passage is described by Böhler as most wretched. Their supply of provisions was insufficient, and the captain and crew were by no means courteous. Before the conclusion of the voyage they were content to have a quarter of a pound of bread per day, while their water-casks were quite exhausted. The passengers responded nobly to an appeal to their private resources, and seasonable supplies of fish were also procured.

Among other nautical *memorabilia* they describe a splendid rainbow in a cloudless sky,—a perfect cloud of beautiful flying fishes,—and a waterspout of most extraordinary dimensions. The tedium of the voyage was beguiled by the rich and varied psalmody of the German Church, in which the pilgrims greatly delighted, accompanied by trombones, on which they were accomplished performers; while their devotions were observed with exemplary regularity, and proved to be seasons of great unction and power.

Very welcome was the cry of " Land a-head ! " and great was their joy when they united with Böhler in appropriate thanksgivings in the chapel of the Brethren in New York. Within four days of their arrival we find Böhler at Bethlehem, where his appearance was so unexpected that he entered the room without being perceived by any one. The mutual joy of the Bishop and his former flock may be more easily conceived than described. Their hearts clave unto each other; and it requires no extraordinary discernment to perceive that around that lovely spot his best affections clustered in their richest growth.

Böhler's episcopate in America was commenced under circumstances similar to those which had

existed in England. He found the estates of the
settlement much embarrassed. Heavy mortgages
had been contracted under pressure, or in fear of
imaginary dangers, and their foreclosure appeared
inevitable. The zeal of the Brethren had outrun
their prudence ; or, what is more probable, the
management had been inefficient and unwise. The
peril was extreme ; and the results of many years of
self-denying toil might have been swept away in a
moment by the remorseless creditors. The case
required extraordinary efforts, while the conduct of
the delicate negotiations needed much of the wisdom
which cometh from above, and the help which Omni-
potence alone can supply. Many sleepless nights
were passed by the devoted Bishop ; but his calm
and unfaltering trust in God was in this, as in other
instances, honoured by the great Master, and the
property of the Church was preserved in the possession of the Brethren.

Here we may briefly glance at the prominent
features of his extensive diocese. He had to take
charge of institutions requiring a vigilant eye, a
wise discretion, and the union of uncompromising
fidelity and great tenderness in the administrator.
The Churches placed beneath his care had been
gathered from many tribes; and their shades of
colour and varieties of physical character must have
been remarkable.

Among the members of these Churches were
chiefs who had kindled the big fire of the council-

chamber; prepared or handled the black wampum; brandished the tomahawk, or "lifted the hatchet;" sounded the key-note of the war-whoop, so terrific to the ear of a foe; or led the dance which preceded scenes of savage warfare, the mere allusion to which awakens the shudder of humanity.

The candidates for baptism comprised persons adorned with the tails of foxes, or with the skins of serpents intertwined in their hair; who were decorated with magnificent plumes of feathers, their cheeks tattooed with the forms of birds, animals, and reptiles, and their faces covered with black and vermilion.

The labours of the evangelists had been conducted amid privations and toils of the most exhausting nature. The howling wolves had to be driven from their encampment with blazing torches; occasionally scenes like those portrayed in " The Prairie on Fire " were witnessed; and on one occasion the flame of their burning property was distinctly seen across the Blue Mountains, at a distance of more than thirty miles.

They had to satisfy the pangs of hunger on bilberries, chestnuts, and wild honey. Their animal food was procured by the chase,—as they shot a bird, or brought down the deer; and, in one instance, they made a meal of poor Bruin, who had fallen into their hands. In one of their journeys the hungry cries of the children were appeased by peeling the chestnut-trees of their bark, and allow-ing them to suck the saccharine juice concealed beneath the rind.

They were in continual perils from the treacherous tribes, for whose temporal and spiritual welfare they were unceasingly solicitous. They had to cross the rapid rivers, to ascend the lofty mountains; and, passing by the remains of villages once populous, whose desolation told of tribal strife so fierce that probably no survivor had been spared to tell the tale, they had to thread their weary way among the lengthening forests, where no European had ever trod.

Seldom have the records of the Church displayed a nobler specimen of heroic courage or calm submission than that witnessed in the death of the devoted wife of Senseman, who perished by burning, in a murderous assault by the Indians. Her husband witnessed the horrid sight, but was unable to render any aid, as standing with folded arms amid the raging flames, she exclaimed, " 'Tis all well, dear Saviour."

Amid scenes so exciting, and surrounded by events which taxed his mental and physical powers to the utmost, Böhler pursued his holy mission. He could adopt the language of the great apostle: " In journeyings often, in perils of waters, in perils of robbers, in perils by the heathen, in perils in the city, in perils in the wilderness, in perils in the sea, in perils among false brethren; in weariness and painfulness, in watchings often, in hunger and thirst, in cold,"—perhaps we might also add, " and nakedness ; "—"beside those things that are without, that which cometh upon me daily, the care of all the churches."

Nor need he have felt any misgiving in appropriating the apostolical declaration, " Giving no offence in anything, that the ministry be not blamed : but in all things approving ourselves as the ministers of God, in much patience, in afflictions, in necessities, in distresses,......in imprisonments, in tumults, in labours, in watchings, in fastings ; by pureness, by knowledge, by longsuffering, by kindness, by the Holy Ghost, by love unfeigned, by the word of truth, by the power of God, by the armour of righteousness on the right hand and on the left, by honour and dishonour, by evil report and good report: as deceivers, and yet true; as unknown, and yet well known ; as dying, and, behold, we live ; as chastened, and not killed; as sorrowful, yet alway rejoicing ; as poor, yet making many rich ; as having nothing, and yet possessing all things."

But rich and abundant has been the spiritual harvest gathered from the precious seed which the Moravian evangelists oft watered with their tears ; and the beautiful vale of Wyoming, rendered classic by the muse of Campbell, is still more distinguished by the Christian temples and institutions which adorn the banks of the Susquehanna, as it rolls along,

" Wearing its robe of silver like a bride."

The impressions of Mrs. Sigourney are thus recorded : " The settlements of Bethlehem and Nazareth in Pennsylvania, inhabited by the Moravians, are truly interesting to strangers.   They exhibit peculiar indications of order, industry, and comfort ; and the expanse of ten miles which divides them is marked by neat and careful cultivation.   The beauty of the groves was particularly obvious ; kept free from underwood, and carpeted with fresh green turf, scarcely defaced by a scattered leaf or spray.   The banks of the Lehigh, at Bethlehem, are overshadowed by large, lofty, umbrageous trees, which add much to the romantic character of the landscape. We visited the school for girls, which enjoyed a high reputation in early times, when our country could boast but few institutions for the education of females.   The different classes seemed in perfect order, and the countenances of the pupils evinced contentment and happiness.......The spacious church at Bethlehem is adorned with the portraits of many missionaries, the sect of the Moravians having very early entered the field of Missionary labour, and wrought there with tireless and self-denying zeal.

" Our approach to Nazareth, which was from the beautiful region of Wyoming, through Bear-Creek, Stoddartsville, &c., was rendered striking by passing, at the hour of sunset, the base of a lofty mountain, from whose empurpled summit rays of crimson and gold went streaming up the horizon in prolonged and magnificent coruscations.   Nazareth has a school for boys, which was well filled, and maintained a good reputation. Its members seemed to enjoy that health of body, and those salubrious moral influences, without which the intellectual gains of the young are but a mockery."

The honourable career of Böhler was not unchequered by adverse events; as when, owing to some unexplained cause, his return to Europe was delayed after the return of Spangenberg to America, which produced a state of mental depression so deep as materially to affect his health. But, regaining his wonted elasticity, he visited the infant settlement at Bethabara, North Carolina, and organized a church there.

Itinerating through several parts of the province, he returned to Bethlehem, and in a few days was on his way to New York. There he remained until March, 1755, having the pastoral charge of that important church.

Now, as ever, "in labours more abundant," his lengthened journeys recall the honest boast of the apostle, that "from Jerusalem round about unto Illyricum" he "had fully preached the Gospel of Christ." Nor were these evangelistic toils unblessed to the conversion of many. He was an eminently awakening preacher, and the spoils of his spiritual warfare were extensive and valuable.

At the conclusion of a Synod held at Warwick, the arrival of the "Irene" was announced, and Böhler gladly responded to the call to attend a General Synod at Berthelsdorf, in Saxony. His last

visit to America had occasioned much mental per-
turbation, and it is to be feared he was exposed to
vexatious annoyances. The allusions to these events
in his letters are cautious and guarded; but it is
evident that his spirit was deeply wounded. Might
the wise counsels of Dr. Cotton Mather have been
inappropriate? "If calumnious quills have publicly scratched you,—an respondendum semper
calumniis? No. Look as far back as two thousand
years ago, and you will find even a Plato giving a
pattern to a Christian in his declining to take any
notice of the invectives which a Xenophon had used
towards him. It may be, the scribblers are such
sorry scoundrels, and such vile children of Sheth,
that it is beneath you to let them know that you
have so much as read their follies. Or be they what
they will, for the most part the best way will be to
shine on regardless of what the bats and owls may
mutter against you. Or if that metaphor be too
sublime, let me say, at least, as the moon among
the lesser fires, keep a steady face, walking in
your brightness, notwithstanding the unregardable
allatrations of your adversaries."

He was accompanied to New York by his wife,
who, as she bade him adieu on board the "Mesopo-
tamia," obtained this well-earned tribute to her
memory in his diary, "Here we bade each other
farewell; and this leave-taking, and especially the
noble bearing of my Elizabeth, will remain impressed
upon my heart as long as I live." The passage to

Europe was stormy and dangerous. They reached
the Orkneys on the day of the great earthquake at
Lisbon. It is not improbable that the terrible convulsion which laid that noble city in ruins was extensively felt, as terrific storms ensued which drove them
through the passage into the North Sea. Very
perilous and exciting were the seven successive days,
when, passing by the beautiful ruins of Tynemouth
Priory, where many a gallant vessel has perished,
they proceeded along the " coaly Tyne " to Newcastle,
and then with all convenient speed to the settlement
at Fulneck.

Welcome indeed must have been the retirement of
that lovely spot, with its noble terrace and inviting
grounds ; and very pleasant the society of the venerable elders and their devoted flock. But other
duties forbade Böhler's lengthened stay to enjoy the
rest and relaxation needed to repair the exhausting
effects of unceasing toils and cares. He reached
Herrnhut on the 20th of December, and proceeded
at once to Zinzendorf's mansion at Berthelsdorf,
where he had a lengthened interview with the
Count.

The Synod which was held in June, 1756,
was of no ordinary importance. A review of the
propositions established and enforced reminds us,
very forcibly, of the terse and graphic paragraphs
contained in the Minutes of the early Conferences
between the Wesleys and others at the Foundery in
London.

This was Böhler's final interview with Zinzendorf; and the last entry in his autobiography bears the date of June 1st, 1756. Authentic records of the rest of his life are at present meagre; so that our remaining notices are brief. He remained in Germany six months. Then, undeterred by former disasters and sorrows, and " not counting his life dear unto him," he crossed the Atlantic for the seventh time, and was for eight years the efficient coadjutor and assistant of Spangenberg.

In 1764 Böhler bade a final adieu to America, a country where he had prosecuted his sacred duties with a zeal worthy of apostolic times ; where, also, some of his severest trials had been endured, and his noblest conquests achieved. He had the pleasure of seeing the settlements which he had founded multiplying their converts, exerting an influence of the most hallowed character over extensive districts, and presenting abundant hope of continued growth and prosperity. The proud and haughty savage had been subdued by the omnipotent power of Divine grace ; and chiefs, whose names had been the terror of the nation, had been seen to bow in deep humility and grateful love as they commemorated the sacrificial death of the Son of God. Had he a presentiment of his approaching dissolution? If so, the last glance at his beloved Bethlehem and Nazareth, and the parting address to the converts whom he had begotten in the Lord, would have furnished a fitting counterpart to the scene recorded at Miletus, and not unworthy of the purest ages of the Church.

The Marienborn Synod assembled under circumstances of deep solemnity. Zinzendorf had been removed to the "general assembly" of the redeemed; but, while deeply mourning his departure, the brethren addressed themselves hopefully to their new and responsible duties. Böhler was now elected as one of the "Directors," to whom the executive administration of the Church was intrusted; and was subsequently a member of the "Unity's Elders' Conference," the supreme ruling power and court of appeal in the " *Unitas Fratrum* ;" and in this important office he nobly earned the "double honour" awarded to those who "rule well" in the Lord's house.

It was during one of his official visits to England that he was removed to the purer society and holier worship of the heavenly state. He was anticipating an early return to Germany, and the arrangements for the journey were completed. He preached on April 19th, 1775, in the Fetter-lane chapel, on 2 Tim. ii. 8: "Remember that Jesus Christ of the seed of David was raised from the dead according to my Gospel;" and then the end drew near. On the 26th he paid an edifying visit to a member of his Church, and returned to his room in time to prepare for the evening service. Sitting down in his arm-chair, he adjusted his spectacles, and began to concentrate his thoughts upon the "watchword,"* which was to form the theme of his address. Suddenly a new sensation pervaded one half of his entire frame; and in a moment more his right hand forgot its cunning, his right side became utterly helpless, and his left eye no longer shot forward its wonted glances of intelligence. Paralysis had done its work. The power of speech, which he had used so well through a long and laborious life, in preaching "the glorious Gospel of the blessed God," had fled. His mental faculties were overcast by a cloud, which was not to be removed until he should reach a brighter and serener world than ours.

Surrounded by the members of the Elders' Conference, and other· devoted friends, whose presence he now and then acknowledged by a look of recognition slightly beaming in his right eye, or the gentle pressure of the left hand, the tide of life calmly and painlessly ebbed away. To those assembled in the chamber of death the Saviour's presence was graciously and eminently manifested. They filled the room with the sound of solemn melody, as they sang appropriate hymns. Then they adored in solemn silence the goodness of Him who had safely brought their departing brother to the bourn of life; and anon they offered fervent prayers for the special support and final triumph of one whom they tenderly regarded as a "father" in Israel.

* The Moravian "watchword" is prepared by the authorities, and, being published in advance, engages the attention of each member of the Church throughout the world.

At length, at half-past five on the morning of the 27th, in the presence of many of his brethren, and attended by the gentle ministry of her whose life-long affection and fidelity he so much prized, the last breath was drawn. The passage of the dark-flowing river was neither difficult nor protracted, and, escorted by the shining ones, the spirit entered the world of the holy. And now the weary pilgrim is at rest! The faithful warrior has more than gained the victory! His wise counsels, his evangelistic toils and countless anxieties, are at an end; and he waits for the day when, from the lips of the Saviour revealed in glory, he will receive the welcome plaudit, "Well done, good and faithful servant; enter thou into the joy of thy Lord."

Four days more, and his body, which had been the temple of the Holy Ghost, was removed to the cemetery attached to Lindsey House, Chelsea. A congregation of nearly eight hundred persons, including the officers and members of the Fetter-lane congregation, as well as many strangers, witnessed the funeral obsequies. The Rev. Benjamin La Trobe read the impressive service of the Moravian Church. The triumphant chorales, accompanied by instrumental music, by which the Brethren celebrate the addition of another member to the glorified church, were sung. A solemn discourse, founded upon Luke xii. 40, "Be ye therefore ready also: for the Son of man cometh at an hour when ye think not," and interspersed with many tender recollections of the departed, closed the solemn service; and the remains of this man of God were deposited in their final resting-place, until the resurrection morning.

The associations of that quiet spot where he slumbers are deeply affecting, recalling many honoured names, and imparting to it a melancholy charm. Surrounded by the dust of some of his companions in study at Jena, and many of the associates of his hallowed toil in this and other lands, his grave is only distinguished by a lowly stone, bearing the following inscription :—

PETRUS BOHLER,

A BISHOP OF THE UNITAS FRATRUM,

DEPARTED, APRIL 27TH, 1775,

IN THE SIXTY-THIRD YEAR OF HIS AGE.

But let us rise from the contemplation of the tomb, and its mournful surroundings, and fix our thoughts on that holier region where, far from the imperfections and sorrows of the earthly church, Böhler and Zinzendorf, the Wesleys and Fletcher, and a countless host who have trod in the steps of their faith, shall unite, without one dissonant note, in ascriptions of "blessing, and honour, and glory, and power, unto Him that sitteth upon the throne, and unto the Lamb for ever!"

LONDON:
PRINTED BY WILLIAM NICHOLS,
46, HOXTON SQUARE.

RECENT PUBLICATIONS,

OF THE

WESLEYAN CONFERENCE OFFICE.

------------◦┊◦◦◦┊◦------------

Recollections of My Own Life and Times. By Thomas Jackson. Edited by the Rev. B. Frankland, B.A. With an Introduction and Postscript by G. Osborn, D.D. With a Portrait. Crown 8vo. Price 8s. 6d.

Memorials of the Rev. Francis A. West. Being a Selection from his Sermons and Lectures. With a Biographical Sketch by one of his Sons, and Personal Recollections by the Rev. B. Gregory. Crown 8vo. Price 4s.

Class-Meetings in Relation to the Design and Success of Methodism. By the Rev. S. W. Christophers. Crown 8vo. Price 3s.

A Man of God ; or, Providence and Grace Exemplified in a Memoir of the Rev. Peter M'Owan. Compiled chiefly from his Letters and Papers. By the Rev. John M'Owan. Edited by G. Osborn, D.D. Crown 8vo. Price 5s.

Tamil Wisdom ; Traditions concerning Hindu Sages, and Selections from their Writings. By the Rev. Edward Jewitt Robinson. With an introduction by the late Rev. Elijah Hoole, D.D. And a Frontispiece, from a Madras Picture, of "Tiru Valluvar." Crown 8vo. Price 3s.

> "We warmly recommend the book. . . . To thoughtful Christian men these translations will give an insight into the mind and culture to be found among the people."—*Methodist Recorder.*

How to Pray and What to Pray For. An Exposition of the Lord's Prayer and Christ's Introductory Sayings. By the Rev. Edward Jewitt Robinson. Crown 8vo. Price 5s.

> "A backbone of sound theology runs through the treatise, while in every chapter questions of experience and practice are treated with the incisive vigour of a critical and ardent intellect."—*London Quarterly Review.*

For Ever: An Essay on Eternal Punishment. By the
Rev. MARSHALL RANDLES. Second Edition, Revised and Enlarged.
Crown 8vo. Price 4s.
> "A valuable contribution toward the sound scriptural settlement
> of this much-vexed question."—*London Quarterly Review.*

Ecclesiastical Principles and Polity of the Wesleyan
Methodists. The whole compiled by WILLIAM·PEIRCE, and revised
by FREDERICK J. JOBSON, D.D. Third Edition. Royal 8vo., cloth, 15s.;
half morocco, cloth sides, 20s.
> This work contains a correct Transcript of all the published Laws
> and Regulations of the Wesleyan Methodist Connexion, from its
> first organization to the present time, and affords full and authentic
> information on the History, Discipline, and Economy of Methodism.

COMMENTARIES, DICTIONARIES, &c.,
ILLUSTRATIVE OF THE HOLY SCRIPTURES.

Aids to Daily Meditation: being Practical Reflections
and Observations on a Passage of Scripture for each Day in the Year.
Crown 8vo., cloth, red edges. Price 5s.

The Holy Bible: with Notes, Critical, Explanatory, and
Practical. By the Rev. JOSEPH BENSON. With Maps and a Portrait of
the Author. Six Volumes, Imperial 8vo., cloth, red edges. Price £3 3s.
Sold also in Separate Volumes, cloth, red edges. Price 10s. 6d. each.

A Biblical and Theological Dictionary: Illustrative of
the Old and New Testament.' By the Rev. JOHN FARRAR. With a Map
of Palestine and numerous Engravings. Crown 8vo. Price 3s. 6d.

An Ecclesiastical Dictionary: Explanatory of the His-
tory, Antiquities, Heresies, Sects, and Religious Denominations of the
Christian Church. By the Rev. JOHN FARRAR. Crown 8vo. Price 5s.

The Proper Names of the Bible; their Orthography,
Pronunciation, and Signification. With a brief Account of the Principal
Persons, and a Description of the principal Places. By the Rev. JOHN
FARRAR. 18mo. Price 1s. 6d.

A Commentary on the Old and New Testament; containing copious notes, Theological, Historical, and Critical; with Improvements and Reflections. By the Rev. JOSEPH SUTCLIFFE, M.A. Imperial 8vo., cloth, marbled edges. Price 12s. 6d.

A Biblical and Theological Dictionary, Explanatory of the History, Manners, and Customs of the Jews, and Neighbouring Nations. With an Account of the most remarkable Places mentioned in Sacred Scripture; An Exposition of the principal Doctrines of Christianity; and Notices of Jewish and Christian Sects and Heresies. By the Rev. RICHARD WATSON. Royal 8vo., cloth, red edges. Price 12s. 6d.

An Exposition of the Gospels of St. Matthew and St. Mark, and of some other detached parts of Scripture. By the Rev. RICHARD WATSON. Demy 8vo. Price 6s. 12mo. Price 3s. 6d.

The New Testament, with Explanatory Notes. By the Rev. JOHN WESLEY. With the Author's last Corrections.
Pocket Edition. 18mo. Price 2s.
Large-Type Edition. 8vo. Price 4s.
Library Edition, fine paper. Demy 8vo. Price 6s.

An Exposition of St. Paul's Epistle to the Romans. By the Rev. HENRY W. WILLIAMS. Crown 8vo. Price 6s.

An Exposition of the Epistle to the Hebrews. By the Rev. HENRY W. WILLIAMS. Crown 8vo. Price 6s.

The Incarnate Son of God: or, the History of the Life and Ministry of the Redeemer; arranged, generally, according to Greswell's Harmony of the Gospels. By the Rev. HENRY W. WILLIAMS. Crown 8vo. Price 4s.

Scripture compared with Scripture. A Plan for Daily Bible Reading throughout the Year. Arranged by E. G. C. Price 6d.; limp cloth, gilt edges, 8d.

THEOLOGY.

Bunting (J.)   Sermons by the Rev. Jabez Bunting, D.D.
Two Volumes. Crown 8vo., cloth, red edges. Price 10s. 6d.
Volume Two is sold separately. Price 3s. 6d.

Dunn (L. R.)   The Mission of the Spirit; or the Office
and Work of the Comforter in human Redemption. By the Rev. LEWIS
R. DUNN, Minister of the Methodist Episcopal Church, U.S. Edited
by the Rev. JOSEPH BUSH. Crown 8vo. Price 2s.

Edmondson (J.)   Sermons on Important Subjects; with
an Introduction by the Rev. T. JACKSON. Two Volumes. Crown 8vo.
Price 6s.

Fletcher (J.)   An Appeal to Matter of Fact and Com-
mon Sense; or, a Rational Demonstration of Man's Corrupt and Lost
Estate. By the Rev. JOHN FLETCHER. 12mo. Price 2s.

Fletcher (J.)   Five Checks to Antinomianism.   By the
Rev. JOHN FLETCHER. 12mo. Price 4s. 6d.

Fletcher (J.)   The Works of the Rev. John Fletcher;
with his Life, by the Rev. JOSEPH BENSON. Complete in Nine Volumes.
12mo. Price £1 11s. 6d.

Hannah (J.)   Introductory Lectures on the Study of
Christian Theology: with Outlines of Lectures on the Doctrines of
Christianity. By the late Rev. JOHN HANNAH, D.D.; to which is pre-
fixed a Memoir of Dr. Hannah, by the Rev. W. B. POPE. Crown 8vo.
Price 6s.

Jackson (T.)   The Duties of Christianity; theoretically
and practically considered. By the Rev. THOMAS JACKSON. Second
Edition. Crown 8vo. Price 4s.

Jackson (T.)   The Institutions of Christianity, exhibited
in their Scriptural Character and Practical Bearing. By the Rev.
THOMAS JACKSON. Crown 8vo. Price 5s.

Jackson (T.) *The Providence of God, viewed in the Light*
of Holy Scripture. By the Rev. THOMAS JACKSON. New Edition, with
Improvements. Crown 8vo. Price 4s.

Jackson (T.) *The Christian armed against Infidelity.*
A Collection of Treatises in Defence of Divine Revelation. Foolscap
8vo. Price 2s.

McAfee (D.) *The Pillar and Ground of the Truth.*
Twelve Sermons on the Fundamental Truths of Christianity. By the
Rev. DANIEL MCAFEE. With a Preface, by the Rev. WILLIAM ARTHUR,
M.A. Crown 8vo. With Portrait. Price 6s.

Pope (W. B.) *The Kingdom and Reign of Christ.*
Twenty-one Discourses delivered in the Chapel of the Wesleyan Theological Institution, Didsbury. By the Rev. WILLIAM B. POPE, Theological Tutor. Foolscap 8vo. Price 5s.

Prest (C.) *The Witness of the Holy Spirit.* *By the Rev.*
CHARLES PREST. Third Edition. Crown 8vo., cloth, red edges. Price 3s.

Thomas (J. W.) *The Lord's Day; or, the Christian*
Sabbath: its History, Obligation, Importance, and Blessedness. By
the Rev. JOHN WESLEY THOMAS. Crown 8vo. Price 3s. 6d.

Treffry (R.) *Inquiry into the Doctrine of the Eternal*
Sonship of our Lord Jesus Christ. By the Rev. RICHARD TREFFRY, Jun.
Crown 8vo. Price 6s.

Treffry (R.) *The Atonement viewed in Relation to*
Scripture and Reason. In a series of Letters to a Friend. By the Rev.
RICHARD TREFFRY, Jun. 18mo. Price 2s.

Treffry (R.) *The Infidel's Own Book.* A Statement of
some of the Absurdities resulting from the Rejection of Christianity.
By the Rev. RICHARD TREFFRY, Jun. 18mo. Price 2s. 6d.

Watson (R.) *Sermons and Sketches of Sermons.* By
the Rev. RICHARD WATSON.
   Three Volumes, demy 8vo. Price 18s.
   Three Volumes, post 8vo. Price 10s. 6d.

Watson (R.) *Theological Institutes; or, a View of the*
Evidences, Doctrines, Morals, and Institutions of Christianity.
Rev. RICHARD WATSON.
   Three Volumes, demy 8vo. Price 18s.
   Four Volumes, royal 18mo. Price 14s.

Watson (R.) The Works of the Rev. Richard Watson.
With his Memoirs by the Rev. THOMAS JACKSON.
> Thirteen Volumes, demy 8vo. Price £3 18s.
> Thirteen Volumes, post 8vo. Price £2 5s. 6d.

Wesley (J.) Sermons on Several Occasions. By the
Rev. JOHN WESLEY, M.A. With a Life of the Author by the Rev. JOHN
Beecham, D.D.
> Three Vols., crown 8vo. Price 7s. 6d.
> Fine Edition, three Vols., crown 8vo. Price 10s. 6d.
> Library Edition, three Vols., demy 8vo. Price 18s.

Wesley (J.) The Prose Works of the Rev. John Wesley,
M.A. Edited by the Rev. THOMAS JACKSON. This Edition contains all
the Latest Corrections of the Author; and includes the Life of Mr.
Wesley by the Rev. JOHN BEECHAM, D.D.
> Library Edition, Fourteen Volumes, demy 8vo. Price £4 4s.
> Cheap Edition, Fourteen Volumes, post 8vo. Price £2 2s.

BIOGRAPHY.

Agar (B.) Memoirs of Mrs. Benjamin Agar, of York;
With Extracts from her Diary and Correspondence. By the Rev. LUKE
H. WISEMAN, M.A., Author of "Christ in the Wilderness," "Men of
Faith," &c. Crown 8vo. Price 2s. 6d.

Alpine Missionary (The); or, the Life of J. L. Rostan,
Missionary Pastor in France, Switzerland, and the Channel Isles. By
the Rev. MATTHEW LELIEVRE. Translated from the French Edition,
by the Rev. A. J. FRENCH, B.A. With a Portrait. Crown 8vo. Price
3s. 6d.

Bamford (J.) · The Disciple among the Poor : Memorials
of Mr. John Bamford, of Shardlow. By his Son, the Rev. JOHN M.
BAMFORD. Crown 8vo. Price 3s. With Photographic Portrait, 3s. 6d.

Bentley (S.) The Living Sacrifice. A Biographical
Notice of Sarah Bentley, of York. By the Rev. JOHN LYTH. 18mo.
Price 1s.

Bohler, (P.) Memorials of the Life of Peter Bohler,
Bishop of the Church of the United Brethren. By the Rev. J. P.
LOCKWOOD. With an Introduction by the Rev. THOMAS JACKSON; and
with a finely engraved Portrait. Crown 8vo. Price 2s. 6d.

Bramwell (W.) The Christian Minister in Earnest. A
Memoir of the Rev. William Bramwell; containing Extracts from his
Correspondence, and a Delineation of his Personal and Ministerial
Character. By the Rev. THOMAS HARRIS. Royal 18mo., gilt edges.
Price 3s.
    Cheap Edition. Royal 32mo. Price 1s.

Bumby (J. H.) The Life of the Rev. John H. Bumby.
With a brief History of the Progress of the Wesleyan Mission in New
Zealand. By the Rev. ALFRED BARRETT. With a Portrait. 12mo.
Price 3s.

Bunting (William M.) Memorials of. Being Selections
from his Sermons, Letters, and Poems. Edited by the Rev. G. STRINGER
ROWE. With a Biographical Introduction by THOMAS PERCIVAL
BUNTING. Crown 8vo. Price 3s. 6d.

Carvosso (W.) Memoirs of William Carvosso. Written
by himself, and edited by his Son. With a Portrait. Royal 18mo.
Price 2s. 6d.
    Cheap Edition. Royal 32mo. Price 1s.

Clarke (A.) The Life of Dr. Adam Clarke. By the
Rev. Dr. ETHERIDGE. With a Portrait. Post 8vo. Price 3s. 6d.

Coke (T.) The Life of Thomas Coke. By the Rev. Dr.
ETHERIDGE. With a Portrait. Post 8vo. Price 3s. 6d.

Cross (W.) Memoir of the Rev. William Cross, Missionary to the Friendly and Fejee Islands. With a Notice of the
History of the Missions. By the Rev. JOHN HUNT. 18mo. Price 2s.

Cryer (Mrs.) Holy Living; Exemplified in the Life of
Mrs. Mary Cryer, Wife of the Rev. Thomas Cryer, Wesleyan Mission-
ary in India. By the Rev. ALFRED BARRETT. With Vignette Title and
Frontispiece. Foolscap 8vo. Price 3s.

Dixon (T.) The Earnest Methodist. A Memoir of the
late Mr. Thomas Dixon, of Grantham. By his Nephew, the Rev.
JOSEPH DIXON. Foolscap 8vo. With Portrait. Price 2s.

Entwisle (J.)   Memoir of the Rev. Joseph Entwisle: with copious Extracts from his Journals and Correspondence, and Occasional Notices of Contemporary Events in the History of Methodism. By his Son. With a Portrait. Crown 8vo. Price 3s.

Field (J.)   Memoirs of Mr. James Field (of Cork, formerly Serjeant in the Royal British Regiment of Artillery.) By the Rev. R. HUSTON. 18mo. Price 1s. 6d.

Fletcher (J.)   The Life of the Rev. John Fletcher. By the Rev. JOSEPH BENSON. With a Portrait. 12mo. Price 3s. 6d. Cheap Edition. Royal 32mo. Price 1s.

Fletcher (Mrs.)   The Life of Mrs. Fletcher. By the Rev. HENRY MOORE. With a Portrait. Crown 8vo. Price 3s. 6d. Cheap Edition. Royal 32mo. Price 1s.

George (E.)   Memoirs of Elizabeth George. By the Rev. HENRY J. PIGGOTT, B.A. With a Portrait. Crown 8vo. Price 2s. 6d.

Grimshaw (W.), Incumbent of Haworth. By the Rev. R. SPENCE HARDY. Crown 8vo. Price 3s.

Jackson (T.)   Lives of Early Methodist Preachers. Chiefly written by themselves. Edited with an Introductory Essay by the Rev. THOMAS JACKSON. Library Edition, Six Vols. Crown 8vo. Price 18s. Cheap Edition, Six Vols. Foolscap 8vo. Price 9s.

Jackson (T.)   Recollections of My Own Life and Times. By THOMAS JACKSON. Edited by the Rev. B. FRANKLAND, B.A. With an Introduction and Postscript by G. OSBORN, D.D. With a Portrait. Crown 8vo. Price 8s. 6d.

M'Owan (P.)   A Man of God; or, Providence and Grace Exemplified in a Memoir of the Rev. Peter M'Owan. Compiled chiefly from his Letters and Papers. By the Rev. JOHN M'OWAN. Edited by G. OSBORN, D.D. Crown 8vo. Price 5s.

Maxwell (Lady).   The Life of Darcy Lady Maxwell. By the Rev. WILLIAM ATHERTON. With Selections from her Diary and Correspondence. Crown 8vo. Price 3s. 6d.

Miller (W. E.)   Life of the Rev. W. E. Miller. By the Rev. Dr. DIXON. Foolscap 8vo. Price 2s.; limp cloth, 1s. 6d.

Mitchell (Mrs.) *Memoir of Mrs. E. K. Mitchell.* By her
Husband, the Rev. J. MITCHELL. 18mo. Price 1s. 6d.

Mortimer (Mrs.) *Memoirs of Mrs. Elizabeth Mortimer.*
By Mrs. BULMER. Fourth Edition. 18mo. Price 2s. 6d.

Nelson (J.) *The Journal of Mr. John Nelson.* Royal
18mo. Price 1s. 6d. Cheap Edition, royal 32mo. Price 10d.

Newton (R.) *The Life of the Rev. Robert Newton, D.D.*
By the Rev. THOMAS JACKSON. With a Portrait. Foolscap 8vo. Price
2s. 6d.

Newton (Mrs.) *Memorials of the Life of Mrs. Newton,*
Wife of the late Rev. Robert Newton, D.D. By her DAUGHTER. Royal
18mo. Cloth, gilt edges. Price 2s. 6d.

Rogers (Mrs.) *The Experience and Spiritual Letters of*
Mrs. Hester Ann Rogers. 18mo. Price 1s. 6d.
Cheap Edition. Royal 32mo. Price 10d.

Rogers (Mrs.) *The Experience, Letters, and Journal of*
Mrs. Hester Ann Rogers. In one Vol. 18mo., roan, embossed, gilt
edges. Price 3s. 6d.

Smith (J.) *Memoirs of the Life, Character, and Labours*
of the Rev. John Smith. By the Rev. R. TREFFRY, Jun. With an
introductory Essay by the Rev. Dr. DIXON. Royal 18mo. Price 3s.
Cheap Edition, without the Introductory Essay. Price 1s.

Stoner (D.) *Memoirs of the Rev. David Stoner.* By
the Rev. Dr. HANNAH and Mr. WILLIAM DAWSON. With a Portrait.
18mo. Price 2s. 6d.
Cheap Edition. Royal 32mo. Price 1s.

Tackaberry (F.) *The Life and Labours of the Rev.*
Fossey Tackaberry; with Notices of Methodism in Ireland. By the
Rev. R. HUSTON. Second Edition. Crown 8vo. Price 3s.

Taylor (Michael C.) *Memoir of the Rev. M. C. Taylor.*
With Extracts from his Correspondence. By the Rev. B. HELLIER.
Crown 8vo. Price 3s. 6d.

Threlfall (W.) *Memorials of the Rev. W. Threlfall.*
By the Rev. SAMUEL BROADBENT. 18mo. With Portrait. Price 1s. 6d.

Treffry (R.)   Memoirs of the Rev. R. Treffry, Jun.
With Select Remains, consisting of Sketches of Sermons, Essays, and
Poetry. By his Father, the Rev. RICHARD TREFFRY. With a Portrait.
12mo. Price 4s. 6d.

Turner (N.)   The Pioneer Missionary; or, the Life of
the Rev. Nathaniel Turner, Missionary in New Zealand, Tonga, and
Australasia. By his Son, the Rev. J. G. TURNER. Crown 8vo. With
Portrait. Price 5s.

Watson (R.)   Memoirs of the Life and Writings of the
Rev. Richard Watson. By the Rev. THOMAS JACKSON. With a Portrait.
Royal 18mo. Price 3s. 6d. 8vo. Price 6s.

Wesley (C.)   The Life of the Rev. Charles Wesley.
Comprising a Review of his Poetry; Sketches of the Rise and Progress
of Methodism; with Notices of Contemporary Events and Characters.
By the Rev. THOMAS JACKSON. With a Portrait. Royal 18mo. Price
3s. 6d.

Wesley (C.)   The Journal of the Rev. Charles Wesley.
With Selections from his Correspondence and Poetry, and an Intro-
duction by the Rev. THOMAS JACKSON. Two Vols. Royal 18mo.
Price 7s.

Wesley (J.)   The Life of the Rev. John Wesley. By the
Rev. RICHARD WATSON. With a Portrait. Royal 18mo. Price 3s. 6d.

Wesley (J.)   The Journals of the Rev. John Wesley.
Four Vols. 12mo. Price 10s.

Wesley (J.)   His Life and his Work. By the Rev. M.
LELIEVRE. Translated by the Rev. A. J. FRENCH. With a Portrait.
Crown 8vo. Price 3s.

West (F. A.)   Memorials of the Rev. Francis A. West.
Being a Selection from his Sermons and Lectures. With a Biographical
Sketch by one of his Sons, and Personal Recollections by the Rev. B.
GREGORY. Crown 8vo. Price 4s.

Wood (J.)   The Life of the Rev. Joseph Wood. With
Extracts from his Diary. By the Rev. H. W. WILLIAMS. With a
Portrait. Crown 8vo. Price 3s.

NEW BOOKS AND NEW EDITIONS,

SUITABLE FOR SUNDAY-SCHOOL LIBRARIES AND REWARDS.

Bleby (H.) The Stolen Children: A Narrative compiled from Authentic Sources, by the Rev. HENRY BLEBY, Author of "Death Struggles of Slavery." Foolscap 8vo., cloth, gilt edges, with Illustrations. Price 2s. 6d.

Briggs (F. W.) Chequer Alley: A Story of Successful Christian Work. By the Rev. FREDERICK W. BRIGGS. With an Introduction by the Rev. W. ARTHUR, M.A. Ninth Edition. Foolscap 8vo. Price 1s. 6d.

Lightwood (E.) Ancient Egypt: Its Monuments, Wor- ship, and People. By the Rev. EDWARD LIGHTWOOD. Royal 16mo., numerous Illustrations. Price 1s.

Montfort (Lillie.) Incidents in my Sunday-School Life. By LILLIE MONTFORT, Author of "My Class for Jesus." Foolscap 8vo. Price 2s.

Old Truths in New Lights. A Series of Sunday-School Addresses. By W. H. S. Foolscap 8vo. Numerous Illustrations. Price 1s. 6d.

Pearse (M. G.) John Tregenoweth: His Mark. By the Rev. MARK GUY PEARSE. Royal 16mo, cloth. Illustrated. Price 1s.

Tatham (E.) The Dream of Pythagoras, and Other Poems. By EMMA TATHAM. Fifth Edition, with Additional Pieces, and a MEMOIR, by the Rev. B. GREGORY, Author of the "Thorough Business Man," etc. Crown 8vo., cloth. Price 3s. 6d. French Morocco, extra gilt, and gilt edges. Price 7s. 6d.

Thomas (J. W.) The Tower, the Temple, and the Minster: Historical and Biographical Reminiscences of the Tower of London, St. Paul's Cathedral, and Westminster Abbey. By the Rev. J. W. THOMAS. Foolscap 8vo. Illustrated. Price 2s.

Thomas (J. W.) William the Silent: A Biographical Study. By the Rev. J. W. THOMAS. Foolscap 8vo. With Portrait. Price 1s.

Waddy (E.) The Father of Methodism. A Sketch of the Life and Labours of the Rev. JOHN WESLEY, A.M. For Young People. By EDITH WADDY. Foolscap 8vo. Numerous Illustrations. Price 1s. 6d.

Waddy, (E.) A Year with the Wild Flowers. An Introduction to the Study of English Botany. By EDITH WADDY. Royal 16mo. Numerous Illustrations. Price 3s. 6d.

Yeames (J.) Vignettes from English History. By the Rev. JAMES YEAMES. First Series. From the Norman Conqueror to Henry IV. Royal 16mo. Numerous Illustrations. Price 1s.

BOOKS SUITABLE FOR SUNDAY SCHOOL LIBRARIES AND REWARDS.

Adeline. Helen Leslie: or, Truth and Error. By Adeline. 18mo. Price 1s.

Barrett (A.) The Boatman's Daughter. A Narrative for the Learned and Unlearned. 18mo. Price 1s. 4d.

Cubitt (G.) Memorable Men and Memorable Events.
COLUMBUS; or, the Discovery of America.
CORTES; or, the Discovery and Conquest of Mexico.
GRANADA; or, the Expulsion of the Moors from Spain.
PIZARRO; or, the Discovery and Conquest of Peru.
By the Rev. G. CUBITT. 18mo. 1s. each. '

Doncaster (J.) Friendly Hints, addressed to the Youth of Both Sexes, on Mind, Morals, and Religion. By the Rev. JOHN DONCASTER. 18mo. Price 1s. 6d.

Dutch Tiles: Being Narratives of Holy Scripture. With Pictorial Illustrations. For the use of Children. 18mo. Price 2s.

Facts and Incidents Illustrative of the Scripture Doctrines as set forth in the First and Second Catechisms of the Wesleyan Methodists. Second Edition. Crown 8vo. 3s. 6d.

Gems of English Poetry: From Chaucer to the Present Time. Selected by Mrs. MARZIALS. Foolscap 8vo., gilt edges. Price 3s. 6d.

Hartley (J.) Hid Treasures and the Search for Them : being Lectures to Bible Classes. By the Rev. JOHN HARTLEY. Royal 18mo. Price 2s. 6d.

Hay (D.) A Father's Religious Counsels Addressed to his Son at School. By the Rev. DAVID HAY. 18mo. 1s.

Hay (D.) Home: or, the Way to Make Home Happy. By the Rev. DAVID HAY. With an Introduction by the Rev. ALFRED BARRETT. 18mo., gilt edges. Price 1s. 6d.

Huston (R.) Letters on the Distinguishing Excellence of Remarkable Scripture Personages. By the Rev. ROBERT HUSTON. 18mo. Price 1s. 6d.

Huston (R.) Cautions and Counsels Addressed to the Young. Enforced by Illustrations chiefly drawn from Scripture Narratives. 18mo. 1s. 6d.

Hudson (W.) This Transitory Life: Addresses designed to help THOUGHTFUL YOUNG PERSONS correctly to estimate THE PRESENT WORLD and ITS AFFAIRS. By the Rev. WILLIAM HUDSON. Foolscap 8vo. Price 1s. 6d.

Leonard (G.) Life on the Waves; or, Memorials of Captain GEORGE LEONARD. By the Rev. A. LANGLEY, Author of "The Decline and Revival of Religion," etc. With Illustrations. 18mo. Price 1s.

Maunder (G.) Eminent Christian Philanthropists. Brief Biographical Sketches, designed especially as studies for the Young. By the Rev. GEORGE MAUNDER. Royal 18mo. Price 2s. 6d.
This Volume contains Biographical Sketches of

John Howard.	Granville Sharp.	David Nasmith.
Edward Colston.	Thomas Clarkson.	Elizabeth Fry.
Jonas Hanway.	W. Wilberforce.	Thomas F. Buxton.
Richard Reynolds.	J. Butterworth.	Sarah Martin.
Robert Raikes.	William Allen.	

Parker (Mrs.) Annals of the Christian Church. From the First to the Nineteenth Centuries. By MRS. PARKER. With Ten Portraits engraved on Steel. Crown 8vo. Price 3s. 6d.

Sketches from My School-Room. By the Daughter of a
Wesleyan Minister. 18mo. Price 1s.

Smith (B.) Climbing: A Manual for the Young who
desire to rise in Both Worlds. Crown 8vo., cloth extra. Fourth
Edition. Revised and Enlarged. Price 2s. 6d.

Smith (B.) The Power of the Tongue; or, Chapters
for Talkers. By the Rev. BENJAMIN SMITH. Crown 8vo. Price 3s. 6d.

Smith (B.) Sunshine in the Kitchen; or, Chapters for
Maid Servants. By the Rev. BENJAMIN SMITH, Author of "Vice-
Royalty," "Climbing," etc. Crown 8vo. Numerous Illustrations.
Price 3s. 6d.

Smith (B.) Vice-Royalty: or, Counsels respecting
Government of the Heart: addressed especially to Young Men. By
the Rev. BENJAMIN SMITH. Crown 8vo. Price 3s.

Smith (T.) Youths of the Old Testament. By the Rev.
THORNLEY SMITH. 18mo. Price 3s.

Smith (T.) The Holy Child Jesus; or, the Early Life of
Christ: Viewed in connection with the History, Chronology, and
Archæology of the Times. Foolscap 8vo. Price 3s.

Walker (T. H.) Which is Best? or, Cottage Sketches
from Real Life. By the Rev. T. H. WALKER. Royal 18mo. Price 2s. 6d.

Walker (T. H.) Gems of Piety in Humble Life. By the
Rev. T. H. WALKER. Royal 18mo. Price 3s.

Walker (T. H.) Youthful Obligations; or, the Duties
which Young People owe to God, to their Parents, to their Brothers
and Sisters, to Themselves, and to Society. Illustrated by a Large
Number of Appropriate Facts and Anecdotes. Royal 18mo. Price 2s. 6d.

Watson (R.) Conversations for the Young. Designed to
promote the Profitable reading of the Holy Scriptures. Royal 18mo,
Price 3s. 6d.

PUBLISHED AT THE WESLEYAN CONFERENCE OFFICE,

2, CASTLE-STREET, CITY-ROAD, & 66, PATERNOSTER-ROW.

NOW PUBLISHING, IN ROYAL 32MO.

THE METHODIST FAMILY LIBRARY.

THE VOLUMES ALREADY ISSUED ARE:	Paper covers.	Cloth, plain edges.	Cloth, gilt edges.
	s. d.	s. d.	s. d.
1. **The Journal of Mr. JOHN NELSON.** Written by HIMSELF . . . . . . 6d.		0 10	1 0
2. **The Experience and Spiritual Letters** of Mrs. HESTER ANN ROGERS . . . 6d.		0 10	1 0
3. **Sincere Devotion;** Exemplified in the Life of MRS. MARTIN. By the Rev. B. FIELD . 6d.		0 10	1 0
4. **The Life of Mr. SILAS TOLD.** Written by HIMSELF . . . . 6d.		0 10	1 0
5. **A Memoir of Mr. WILLIAM CARVOSSO.** Sixty Years a Methodist Class-Leader. Written by HIMSELF		1 0	1 4
6. **The Life of Mrs. MARY FLETCHER.** Written by HERSELF. Edited by Rev. HENRY MOORE		1 0	1 4
7. **The Life of the Rev. JOHN FLETCHER.** By the Rev. JOSEPH BENSON		1 0	1 4
8. **Prayer: Secret, Social, and Extempore,** being a Treatise on Secret and Social Prayer. By the Rev. R. TREFFRY, Sen.; also A HELP TO EXTEMPORE PRAYER. By the Rev. JOSEPH WOOD		1 0	1 4
9. **A Memoir of the Rev. DAVID STONER;** with Extracts from his Diary and Epistolary Correspondence. By the Rev. JOHN HANNAH and Mr. WILLIAM DAWSON		1 0	1 4
10. **Memoirs of the Life, Character, and Labours** of the REV. JOHN SMITH. By the Rev. RICHARD TREFFRY, Jun.		1 0	1 4
11. **Entire Sanctification Attainable in this Life;** being JOHN WESLEY'S "Plain Account of Christian Perfection;" and FLETCHER'S "Practical Application of the Doctrine to various classes of Christians."		1 0	1 4
12. **The Pioneer Bishop:** The Life and Times of FRANCIS ASBURY. By W. P. STRICKLAND . .		1 0	1 4
13. **A Memoir of JOSEPH B. SHREWSBURY.** By his Father, the Rev. W. J. SHREWSBURY . .		1 0	1 4
14. **The Christian Minister in Earnest:** A Memoir of the REV. WILLIAM BRAMWELL; containing Extracts from his Correspondence, and a Delineation of his Personal and Ministerial Character. By the Rev. THOMAS HARRIS . .		1 0	1 4

"The 'Methodist Family Library' bids fair to be the choicest collection of religious biography, and of popular experimental Divinity in the language. Each book is in itself a gem . . . . . Every Methodist should read and recommend, and, if possible, possess and circulate, these invaluable books."—*Christian Miscellany.*

WESLEYAN CONFERENCE OFFICE,

2, CASTLE-STREET, CITY-ROAD; AND 66, PATERNOSTER-ROW.

COMPLETE IN SIX VOLUMES, FOOLSCAP 8VO., CLOTH, GILT-LETTERED,

PRICE EIGHTEENPENCE EACH,

A CHEAP EDITION

OF

˙LIVES OF

EARLY METHODIST PREACHERS,

WRITTEN CHIEFLY BY THEMSELVES.

EDITED, WITH AN INTRODUCTORY ESSAY, BY THE

REV. THOMAS JACKSON.

CONTENTS OF THE VOLUMES.

VOL. I.—*An Introductory Essay; The Journal of John Nelson: Lives of Christopher Hopper, Thomas Mitchell, Peter Jaco, and John Haine.*

VOL. II.—*Lives of Joseph Cownley, Thomas Olivers, Duncan Wright, Thomas Hanby, Alexander Mather, William Hunter, Robert Roberts, Thomas Payne, and Richard Rodda.*

VOL. III.—*The Life and Death of Mr. Thomas Walsh; and the Lives of John Murlin and John Mason.*

VOL. IV.—*Lives of John Pawson, Sampson Staniforth, Thomas Lee, John Prickard, Jonathan Maskew, Matthias Joyce, and James Rogers.*

VOL. V.—*Lives of Thomas Taylor, John Furz, Thomas Rankin, George Story, William Black, William Ashman, and Richard Whatcoat.*

VOL. VI.—*Lives of John Valton, George Shadford, Jasper Robinson, Thomas Hanson, Robert Wilkinson, Benjamin Rhodes, Thomas Tennant, John Allen, John Pritchard, William Adams;*

AND A GENERAL INDEX TO THE SERIES.

** *The Library Edition, in Six Volumes, Crown 8vo., on Superfine Paper, is still on sale at 3s. per Volume.*

"Few lives are more startling than that of John Nelson, few types of saintly holiness are higher than Thomas Walsh; while Thomas Olivers, John Haime, George Story, and Sampson Staniforth, and a number of other goodly names, represent lives of such intense earnestness, holiness, and activity, as would certainly win them a place in a Catholic calendar of saints, and are so full of glowing adventure that the story of many of them would keep a boy's eyes from winking even late in the night."—*British Quarterly Review.*

WESLEYAN CONFERENCE OFFICE.

2, CASTLE-STREET, CITY-ROAD; AND 66, PATERNOSTER-ROW.